David Decamp Thompson

John Wesley as a Social Reformer

David Decamp Thompson

John Wesley as a Social Reformer

ISBN/EAN: 9783337297503

Printed in Europe, USA, Canada, Australia, Japan

Cover: Foto ©Raphael Reischuk / pixelio.de

More available books at **www.hansebooks.com**

JOHN WESLEY

AS A

SOCIAL REFORMER

BY

D? D. THOMPSON

NEW YORK: EATON & MAINS
CINCINNATI : CURTS & JENNINGS
1898

EATON & MAINS PRESS,
150 Fifth Avenue, New York.

CONTENTS.

JOHN WESLEY

AS A

SOCIAL REFORMER.

I.

THE APOSTLE TO THE POOR.

WITHOUT intention on his part, John Wesley became not only the greatest social reformer of his day, but possibly the greatest in all the history of England. Lecky, in his *History of England in the Eighteenth Century*, in his remarks upon the influences which protected England from the horrors of the revolution which ravaged France, says:

" The evangelical movement, which directly or indirectly originated with Wesley, produced a general revival of religious feeling which has incalculably increased the efficiency of almost every religious body in the community, while at the same time it has not seriously affected party politics. On the great American controversy the leading Methodists were divided, Wesley and Fletcher of Madeley being strongly opposed to the American claims, while the bulk of the

Calvinistic Methodists were inclined to favor them. The many great philanthropic efforts which arose, or at least derived their importance, from the evangelical movement soon became prominent topics of parliamentary debate; but they were not the peculiar glory of any political party, and they formed a common ground on which many religious denominations could co-operate.

"Great, however, as was the importance of the evangelical revival in stimulating these efforts, it had other consequences of, perhaps, a wider and more enduring influence. Before the close of the century in which it appeared a spirit had begun to circulate in Europe threatening the very foundations of society and of belief. The revolt against the supernatural theory of Christianity which had been conducted by Voltaire and the encyclopedists, the material conception of man and of the universe which sprang from the increased study of physical science and from the metaphysics of Condillac and Helvetius, the wild social dreams which Rousseau had clothed in such a transcendent eloquence, the misery of a high-spirited people ground to the dust by unnecessary wars and by partial and unjust taxation, the imbecility and corruption of rulers and priests, had together produced in France a revolutionary spirit, which in its intensity and its proselyting fervor was unequaled since the days of the Reformation. It was soon felt in many lands. Millions of fierce and ardent natures were intoxicated by dreams of impossible equality and of a complete social and political reorganization. Many old abuses perished, but a tone of thought and feeling was introduced into European life which could only lead to anarchy, and at length to despotism, and was beyond all others fatal to that measured and ordered freedom which can alone endure. Its chief characteristics were a hatred of all constituted authority, an insatiable appetite for change, a habit of regarding rebellion as the normal as well as the noblest form of political self-sacrifice, a disdain for all compromise, a contempt for all tradition, a desire to level all ranks and subvert all establishments, a determination to seek progress, not by the slow and cautious amelioration of existing institutions, but by sudden, violent, and revolutionary change. Religion, property, civil authority, and domestic life were all assailed, and doctrines incompatible with the very existence of government were embraced by multitudes with the fervor of a religion. England, on the whole, escaped the contagion. Many causes conspired to save her, but among them a prominent place must, I believe, be given to the new and vehement religious enthusiasm which was at that very time passing through the middle and lower classes of the people, which had enlisted in its service a large proportion of the wilder and more impetuous reformers, and which recoiled with horror from the antichristian tenets that were associated with the revolution in France.''

Wesley's interest in the relief of the poor began while he was at college in Oxford. One of the rigidly observed, if not required, rules of the Holy Club was that its members should give away in relief of the poor all they had left after providing for their own necessities. Wesley in later years wrote: "One of them had thirty pounds a year. He lived on twenty-eight, and gave away forty shillings. The next year, receiving sixty pounds, he still lived on twenty-eight and gave away thirty-two. The third year he received ninety pounds and gave away sixty-two. The fourth year he received one hundred and twenty pounds; still he lived as before, on twenty-eight, and gave to the poor all the rest." This "one" was John Wesley; and the rule here laid down he observed to the end of his life, never spending upon himself more than twenty-eight pounds a year.

The worthy poor and the unworthy found in Mr. Wesley a friend. James Lackington says that "in going the few yards from his study to the pulpit Wesley generally distributed a handful of half crowns to the poor old people of his society." Nor did he confine his care to his own societies. At Bristol, in January, 1740, the severe frost threw many out of work. They had no assistance from the parish, and were in

the last extremity. Wesley made three collections in one week, and was thus able to feed
a hundred, sometimes a hundred and fifty, a
day. The twelve or thirteen hundred French
prisoners at Knowle, near Bristol, whom he visited in October, 1759, also found in him a zealous friend and helper. The evening after his
visit he preached a special sermon, in which he
pleaded for these strangers so earnestly that
about one hundred dollars was raised to provide them with warm clothing. Wesley also
wrote a letter on their behalf to *Lloyd's Evening Post.* The distress they suffered from the
want of clothing was soon abundantly relieved.
In January, 1785, when in his eighty-second
year, Mr. Wesley saw that the poor of the society needed clothes as well as the coals and
bread usually distributed at that season, and
set out to beg a thousand dollars " to clothe
them that needed it most." The London
streets were filled with melting snow, which lay
ankle-deep on the ground, so that his feet were
steeped in snow water nearly from morning to
evening. Five days of such traveling brought
on a severe illness.

As his private income increased his charities increased. He received an allowance of
one hundred and fifty dollars a year from the

London society, and the country societies occasionally paid his traveling expenses, but his private charities were drawn from the income of his Book Room.   For some years previous to 1787 these were not less than five thousand dollars a year, and during his lifetime they amounted to one hundred and fifty thousand dollars.

In his *Earnest Appeal to Men of Reason and Religion*, Wesley devoted some attention to the slanderous charges against Methodists, particularly to those which represented that he and his associates were making money from their preaching; that "their religion was a cloak for covetousness."   To the charge that he had received one thousand three hundred pounds a year (about six thousand five hundred dollars) from the Foundry alone, he replied that the moneys given by the Methodists did not come into his hands at all, but were expended by the stewards in relieving the poor and in buying, erecting, and repairing chapels.   He had, he said, "deliberately thrown up his ease, most of his friends, his reputation, and that way of life which of all others was most agreeable both to his natural temper and education; he had toiled day and night, spent all his time and strength, knowingly destroyed a firm constitution, and was hastening into weakness, pain,

diseases, death—to gain a debt of six or seven
hundred pounds." Addressing himself to his
brother clergy, he asks:

" For what price will you preach (and that with
all your might, not in an easy, indolent, fashionable way) eighteen or nineteen times every
week, and this throughout the year? What
shall I give you to travel seven or eight hundred miles, in all weathers, every two or three
months? For what salary will you abstain
from all other diversions than doing good and
the praising of God? I am mistaken if you
would not prefer strangling to such a life, even
with thousands of gold and silver. . . .

" I will now simply tell you my sense of these
matters, whether you will hear or whether you
will forbear. Food and raiment I have—such
food as I choose to eat and such raiment as I
choose to put on ; I have a place where to lay my
head ; I have what is needful for life and godli-
ness ; and I apprehend this is all the world can
afford. The kings of the earth can give me no
more. For as to gold and silver, I count it dung
and dross ; I trample it under my feet ; I esteem
it just as the mire of the streets. I desire it not ;
I seek it not ; I only fear lest any of it should
cleave to me, and I should not be able to shake
it off before my spirit returns to God. . . . I
will take care (God being my helper) that . . .
none of the accursed thing shall be found in my
tents when the Lord calleth me hence. And
hear ye this, all you who have discovered

the treasures which I am to leave behind me: if I leave behind me ten pounds—above my debts and my books, or what may happen to be due on account of them—you and all mankind bear witness against me that I lived and died a thief and a robber."

Wesley kept his word. Shortly before his death he closed his cashbook with the following words, written in a tremulous hand, so as to be scarcely legible: "For upward of eighty-six years I have kept my accounts exactly; I will not attempt it any longer, being satisfied with the continual conviction that I save all I can and give all I can; that is, all I have."

Wesley's personal charities were only a part of his service for the poor. Early in the history of the Methodist movement he began to utilize his societies for the relief of those in need and the distressed. As early as November, 1740, he had begun systematic relief work, for he writes in his Journal, under date of November 3, 1740: "We distributed, as everyone had need, among the numerous poor of our society, the clothes of several kinds which many who could spare them had brought for that purpose." Under date of Tuesday, November 25, the same year, he wrote in his Journal:

" After several methods proposed for employ-

ing those who were out of business we determined to make a trial of one which several of
our brethren recommended to us. Our aim was,
with as little expense as possible, to keep them
at once from want and from idleness; in order
to do which we took twelve of the poorest, and
a teacher, into the society room, where they
were employed for four months, till spring came
on, in carding and spinning of cotton. And
the design answered. They were employed
and maintained with very little more than the
produce of their own labor."

The demand grew for relief work in London,
and Wesley was obliged to adopt new plans.
He writes, May 7, 1741:

"I reminded the United Society that many
of our brethren and sisters had not needful
food; many were destitute of convenient clothing; many were out of business, and that without their own fault; and many sick and ready
to perish; that I had done what in me lay to
feed the hungry, to clothe the naked, to employ
the poor, and to visit the sick; but was not,
alone, sufficient for these things, and therefore desired all whose hearts were as my heart:
1. To bring what clothes each could spare, to
be distributed among those that wanted most.
2. To give weekly a penny, or what they could
afford for the relief of the poor and sick. My
design, I told them, is to employ for the present all the women who are out of business, and
desire it, in knitting. To these we will first

give the common price for that work they do, and then add according as they need. Twelve persons are appointed to inspect these, and to visit and provide things needful for the sick. Each of these is to visit all the sick within their district, every other day; and to meet on Tuesday evening to give an account of what they have done, and what can be done further."

One of the duties of the stewards in London —whose business was to manage the temporal things of the society—was to send relief to the poor by those appointed to visit them. In the performance of their work they were required to "be frugal," to "give none that asked relief either an ill word or an ill look. Do not hurt them if you cannot help. Expect no thanks from man." The stewards met together at six o'clock every Thursday morning, consulted on the business which came before them, sent relief to the sick as everyone had need, and gave the remainder of what had been contributed each week to those who appeared to be in the most pressing want.

The demand for relief of the needy grew rapidly, and before long the stewards found a great difficulty with regard to the sick. Some were ready to perish before the stewards knew of their illness; and when they did know it was not in their power (being persons generally employed in trade) to visit them so often as they desired. When Mr. Wesley was informed of the situation he called together the entire membership of his society in London, then numbering about four thousand. He explained that it was impossible for the stewards to attend all that were sick in all parts of the city, expressed the desire that the leaders of classes would more carefully inquire, and more constantly inform them, who were sick, and asked, " Who among you is willing, as well as able, to supply this lack of service?" The next morning many willingly offered themselves. Mr. Wesley chose forty-six of those whom he judged to be of the most tender, loving spirit, divided the town into twenty-three parts, and appointed two to visit the sick in each division. It was the business of a visitor "to see every sick person within his district three times a week; to inquire into the state of their souls, and to advise them as occasion may require; to inquire into their disorders and procure advice for them ; to relieve them if they are in want; to do anything for them which he (or she) can do ; to bring in his accounts weekly to the stewards." The visitors were enjoined to observe strictly four rules: " 1. Be plain and open in dealing with souls. 2. Be mild, tender, patient.   3. Be cleanly in all you do for the sick.   4. Be not nice." Mr. Wesley never exhibited greater sagacity than in these four simple rules, especially in the last; for the good effect of much philanthropic personal work is destroyed by the manifest fastidiousness of the doer of the work.

"Upon reflection," writes Mr. Wesley, "I saw how exactly, in this also, we had copied after the primitive Church. What were the ancient deacons? What was Phœbe, the deaconess, but such a visitor of the sick?" Five years later he added: "We have ever since had great reason to praise God for his continued blessing on this undertaking. Many lives have been saved, many sicknesses healed, much pain and want prevented or removed. Many heavy hearts have been made glad, many mourners comforted; and the visitors have found, from Him whom they serve, a present reward for all their labor."

As a result of his efforts to help the sick poor, Mr. Wesley started in connection with the Foundry a medical dispensary—the first free dispensary—after which the Finsbury Dispensary in London, twenty years later, was modeled. The expense of relieving the poor at their homes became so great and the profit was,

comparatively, so little that Mr. Wesley resolved to try whether they might not receive
more benefit in the hospitals. He found hos-
pital treatment to be less expensive; but no
more good was done than before. He asked
the advice of several physicians, for the sick,
but without advantage. He saw the poor
people pining away and several families ruined,
and that without remedy. Finally, as a desper-
ate expedient, he said, "I will prepare and
give them physic myself." This he was competent to do. For more than twenty-five years
he had made anatomy and physic the diversion
of his "leisure hours." His knowledge of medicine was extensive, and his common sense made
it of practical value to many persons. His
Primitive Physic, of which at least twenty-three
editions were issued before his death, grew out
of his medical efforts for the relief of the poor.
Notwithstanding some of his remedies are ab-
surd, an eminent physician pronounced the
book incomparably superior to any other non-
professional work of the same date.

A writer in the Gloucester *Times* tells of a
poor widow who went to Wesley for relief for
her only daughter, who was worn to a shadow
with a distressing cough. Wesley listened to
her story and told her he would see her the

2

next morning. "I am to preach at Tewkes-
bury at twelve o'clock, and shall pass your
eottage." When he came he told the girl: "I
have thought over your state, and will give your
mother a remedy which, with God's blessing, I
trust will do you good; and if God spares my
life I will call upon you when I come this way
again." The medicine led to the girl's complete restoration. In March, 1790, exactly a
year after his first visit, Wesley came again.
He said to the mother: "I see that you are
blessed by God with faculties to use the medi-
cines mercifully given by God for our use, so
that I will instruct you in some further remedies that I have discovered lately; and as my
body will soon be laid with the clods of the
valley, waiting for the resurrection, I shall like
to give you these remedies. Use them for God,
and may he bless you and be with you!" Wesley left with her a small manuscript, in his own
handwriting, containing instructions for the
treatment of prevalent diseases. They won for
the widow the name of "the village doctor."
Her daughter's son became a skillful physician,
and acknowledged that Wesley's remedies,
handed down to him by his grandmother, had
been the most successful he had prescribed during fifty years of professional life.

In the dispensary work Wesley had for assistants an apothecary and a surgeon, and probably sometimes Dr. Whitehead, the local preacher who for many years was his personal physician. He resolved at the start not to go beyond his depth, "but to leave all difficult and complicated cases to such physicians as the patients should choose." All sick persons, whether they belonged to the society or not, were invited by Mr. Wesley to come to him every Friday for such assistance as he could give. In the course of the first five months, at an expense of two hundred dollars, he treated five hundred persons, of whom seventy-one were entirely cured.

Mr. Wesley also started a widows' home. He had observed for some years many who, although not sick, were not able to provide for themselves and had no relatives or friends who took enough interest in their welfare to provide for them. These persons were chiefly feeble, aged widows. So he consulted with the stewards in regard to their relief. All agreed that if the women could be kept in one house it would not only be less expensive to the society but also far more comfortable for them. Wesley had no money with which to begin the work, but he leased two houses near by and fitted them up so that they were warm and clean. He took in as many widows as there was room for, and provided them with things needful for the body. They ate with him and his preachers at the family table. A large part of the expense of this widows' home (commonly called the Poorhouse) was paid for from the weekly contributions of the bands and the collections at the Lord's Supper. Of this work Wesley wrote:

" I have blessed God for this house ever since it began, but lately much more than ever. I honor these widows, for they ' are widows indeed.' So that it is not in vain that, without any design of so doing, we have copied after another of the institutions of the apostolic age. I can now say to all the world, ' Come and see how these Christians love one another.' "

For some time Mr. Wesley was much concerned over the number of children who were like "a wild ass's colt," because their parents could not afford to send them to school. Others of whom he knew were sent to school, but while they learned at least to read and write they also learned, wrote Mr. Wesley, " all kinds of vice at the same time, so that it had been better for them to have been without their knowledge than to have bought it at so dear a price." So Mr. Wesley determined to have them taught in his own house, "that they might have an opportunity of learning to read, write, and cast accounts (if no more) without being under almost a necessity of learning heathenism at the same time." Into his school were gathered about sixty children over six years of age, the parents of most of whom were too poor to pay for their schooling. As many as were in need were also provided with clothes. The expense was chiefly defrayed by voluntary contributions. Rules were laid down for the government of the children and rigidly observed. All were required to be present at the morning sermon. The school hours were from six to twelve and from one to five. There were no playdays. "A happy change," remarks Mr. Wesley, "was soon observed in the children, both with regard to their tempers and behavior."

In the course of his labors Mr. Wesley found many who were not, strictly speaking, so poor that they needed alms, but yet frequently were in want of a present supply of money. Some of these persons were in business, and a small loan for a few weeks or months would tide them over difficulty. But there was no one of whom they could borrow, except the pawnbroker, and to place themselves in his debt was to almost abandon hope. Wesley resolved to try in some way to help such persons. So he devised the

scheme of a loan fund. This was started in
1746, about one hundred and fifty years before
a similar scheme was begun by philanthropic
gentlemen in New York. After deciding to
try his scheme Mr. Wesley went from one end
of London to the other and exhorted those who
had an abundance of this world's goods to as-
sist their needy brethren. Fifty pounds (about
two hundred and fifty dollars) were contributed. This sum was placed in the hands of
two stewards, who were present every Tuesday
morning in order to lend to those who desired
any small sum, not exceeding twenty shillings
(about five dollars), which was to be repaid
within three months. The amount which one
person might borrow was afterward increased to
five pounds (about twenty-five dollars). Under
date of Sunday, January 17, 1748, Mr. Wesley
writes in his Journal:

"I made a public collection toward a lending
stock for the poor. Our rule is to lend only
twenty shillings at once, which is repaid weekly
within three months. I began this about a
year and a half ago. Thirty pounds sixteen
shillings were then collected, and out of this no
less than two hundred and fifty-five persons
have been relieved in eighteen months."

This loan fund, or "lending stock," as an in-
stitution of the Methodist societies continued

for a number of years. Among its benefici-
aries was a cobbler named James Lackington,
who in 1775 borrowed five pounds with which
to start a secondhand book shop in connection
with his shoe shop. This new business grew
more rapidly than his cobbling, and in course
of time he gave up the latter. The book business developed into the largest secondhand
bookstore in London, if not in the world. It
made its proprietor immensely wealthy, and
the year Mr. Wesley died Lackington's profits
from his business amounted to twenty-five thousand dollars.

Such social effort constituted a large part of
the work of Mr. Wesley. It is not surprising
that the historian J. R. Green, in his *History
of the English People*, should say: "The Methodists themselves were the least result of the
Methodist revival. . . . The noblest result of
the religious revival was the steady attempt,
which has never ceased from that day to this,
to remedy the guilt, the ignorance, the physical suffering, the social degradation of the prof-
ligate and the poor." A most directly beneficial
result, however, was the inspiration it gave to
those who bestowed their service and their
money.

II.

INFLUENCE UPON THE SOCIAL LIFE OF ENGLAND.

REV. W. MOORE EDE, M.A., rector of Gateshead, in his Hulsean Lectures for 1895 on " The Attitude of the Church to Some of the Social Problems of Town Life," said :

" The man who did most to reform the social life of England in the last century was John Wesley. His appeal was direct ; it was an appeal to the individual ; his aim was to reach the heart and conscience of each man in the crowds which gathered round him. His words were the instrument whereby men were brought to a sense of the sinfulness of their lives and the desire quickened in them to live henceforth more as children of God. His converts were for the most part among the poorest, the most degraded ; as among the early converts of the Church, 'not many mighty, not many noble' were called. How low they had sunk is evident from the observations in his diary, and the need he found for directions as to destruction of vermin. Those whom his appeal reached became changed characters, and the changed character soon expressed itself in changed surroundings ; the homes of the Methodists were cleaner than those of their neighbors, their children were

cared for and clad, they set about improving
their social condition in many ways ; they were
thrifty, and the training they gained in manag-
ing their religious societies, and the develop-
ment of their character which resulted, enabled
them to take a leading part in those self-help
associations—Friendly Societies, Trade Unions,
and Cooperative Societies—which have done so
much to elevate and improve the wage-earning
classes."

This transformation in the personal character
of Mr. Wesley's followers and in the social condition of the kingdom was not accomplished
in a day, or a year, or a decade.   Day after
day, year after year, by exhortation in private
conversation, in letters, in class meetings, in
sermons, in pamphlets, and in books, Mr. Wesley was continually, and in the plainest and
most forcible language, urging his followers to
the pursuance of a course of conduct such as
became a follower of Christ.   In his delineation
of "the character of a Methodist" written in
1739, he says :

" He knows that vice does not lose its nature
though it becomes ever so fashionable, and re-
members that 'every man is to give an account
of himself to God.'   He cannot, therefore, 'follow ' even 'a multitude to do evil.'   He cannot 'fare sumptuously every day,' or 'make
provision for the flesh to fulfill the lusts thereof.'

He cannot 'lay up treasures upon the earth' any more than he can take fire into his bosom. He cannot 'adorn himself,' on any pretense, 'with gold or costly apparel.' He cannot join in or countenance any diversion which has the least tendency to vice of any kind. He cannot 'speak evil' of his neighbor any more than he can lie either for God or man. He cannot utter an unkind word of anyone, for love keeps the doors of his lips. He cannot speak 'idle words;' 'no corrupt communication' ever 'comes out of his mouth,' as is all that 'which is' not 'good to the use of edifying,' not 'fit to minister grace to the hearers.' But 'whatsoever things are pure, whatsoever things are lovely, whatsoever things are' justly 'of good report,' he thinks and speaks and acts, 'adorning the Gospel of our Lord Jesus Christ in all things.' Lastly, as he has time he 'does good unto all men;' unto neighbors and strangers, friends and enemies : and that in every possible kind ; not only to their bodies, by 'feeding the hungry, clothing the naked, visiting those that are sick or in prison;' but much more does he labor to do good to their souls, as of the ability which God giveth ; to awaken those that sleep in death ; to bring those who are awakened to the atoning blood, that, 'being justified by faith, they may have peace with God;' and to provoke those who have peace with God to abound more in love and in good works. And he is willing to 'spend and be spent therein,' even 'to be offered up on the sacrifice and service of their faith,' so they may 'all come unto the measure of the stature of the fullness of Christ.'"

Those who professed sanctification (as all were expected to do in time) were enjoined to "Beware of sins of omission; lose no opportunity of doing good in any kind. Be zealous of good works; willingly omit no work, either of piety or mercy. Do all the good you possibly can to the bodies and souls of men. Particularly, 'thou shalt in any wise reprove thy neighbor, and not suffer sin upon him.' Be active. Give no place to indolence or sloth; give no occasion to say, 'Ye are idle, ye are idle.' Many will say so still; but let your whole spirit and behavior refute the slander. Be always employed; lose no shred of time; gather up the fragments, that nothing be lost. And whatsoever thy hand findeth to do, do it with thy might. Be 'slow to speak' and wary in speaking. 'In a multitude of words there wanteth not sin.' Do not talk much; neither long at a time. Few can converse profitably above an hour. Keep at the utmost distance from pious chitchat, from religious gossiping."

The minutest affairs of his people were of interest to him. He instructed them in their domestic as well as religious life. An illustration of the extent to which he would go sometimes is seen in his "Plain Words" to Mr. S., at Armagh, to whom, under date of April 24, 1769, he wrote:

"DEAR BROTHER: I shall now tell you the things which have been more or less upon my mind ever since I have been in the north of Ireland. If you forget them you will be a sufferer, and so will the people; if you observe them it will be good for both.

"1. To begin with little things. If you regard your health, touch no supper, but a little milk or water gruel. This will entirely, by the blessing of God, secure you from nervous disorders; especially if you rise early every morning, whether you preach or no.

"2. Be steadily serious. . . .

"3. In every town visit all you can from house to house. . . .

"4. But on this and every other occasion avoid all familiarity with women. This is deadly poison both to them and you. You cannot be too wary in this respect; therefore begin from this hour.

"5. The chief matter of your conversation, as well as your preaching, should doubtless be the weightier matters of the law. Yet there are several (comparatively) little things which you should earnestly inculcate from time to time; for he that despiseth small things shall fall by little and little. Such are,

"(1) Be active, be diligent; avoid all laziness, sloth, indolence. Fly from every degree, every appearance of it; else you will never be more than half a Christian.

"(2) Be cleanly. In this let the Methodists take pattern by the Quakers. Avoid all nastiness, dirt, slovenliness, both in your person, clothes, house, and all about you. Do not stink above ground. This is a bad fruit of laziness. Use all diligence to be clean; as one says:

"'Let thy mind's sweetness have its operation
Upon thy person, clothes, and habitation.'

"(3) Whatever clothes you have let them be whole; no rents, no tatters, no rags. These are a scandal to either man or woman, being another fruit of vile laziness. Mend your clothes, or I shall never expect you to mend your lives. Let none ever see a ragged Methodist.

"(4) Clean yourselves of lice. These are a proof of uncleanness and laziness; take pains in this. Do not cut off your hair, but clean it and keep it clean.

"(5) Cure yourself and your family of the itch; a spoonful of brimstone will cure you. To let this run from year to year proves both sloth and uncleanness. Away with it at once. Let not the north be any longer a proverb of reproach to all the nation.

"(6) Use no tobacco unless prescribed by a physician. It is an uncleanly and unwholesome self-indulgence, and the more customary it is the more resolutely should you break off from every degree of that evil custom.

"(7) Use no snuff, unless prescribed by a physician. I suppose no other nation in Europe is in such vile bondage to this silly, nasty, dirty custom as the Irish are. But let Christians be in this bondage no longer. Assert your liberty, and that all at once; nothing will be done by degrees. But just now you may break loose, through Christ strengthening you.

"(8) Touch no dram. It is liquid fire. It is sure, though slow, poison. It saps the very springs of life. In Ireland, above all countries in the world, I would sacredly abstain from this, because the evil is so general, and to this, and snuff, and smoky cabins, I impute the blindness which is so exceeding common throughout the nation. . . ."

These were indeed "plain words" to address to one of his preachers; but Mr. Wesley spoke and wrote as plainly to the members of his societies. He was especially severe upon drunkards and smugglers, of whom the number was large. In his printed address to the former, entitled "A Word to a Drunkard," he said :

"1. Are you a man? God made you a man; but you make yourself a beast. Wherein does a man differ from a beast? Is it not chiefly in reason and understanding? But you throw away what reason you have. You strip yourself of your understanding. You do all

you can to make yourself a mere beast ; not a
fool, nor a madman only, but a swine, a poor
filthy swine.   Go and wallow with them in the
mire !   Go, drink on, till thy nakedness be un-
covered, and shameful spewing be on thy
glory ! ''

To those engaged in smuggling, or who ben-
efited by the crime, he addressed himself, in
1767, in a pamphlet entitled *A Word to a
Smuggler*, which he began with the following
paragraphs :

" I. ' What is smuggling ?'   It is the importing, selling, or buying of run goods; that is,
those which have not paid the duty appointed
by law to be paid to the king.

" 1. Importing run goods.   All smuggling
vessels do this with a high hand.   It is the
chief, if not the whole, business of these to
bring goods which have not paid duty.

" 2. Next to these are all sea captains, offi-
cers, sailors, or passengers who import anything without paying the duty which the law
requires.

" 3. A third sort of smugglers are all those
who sell anything which has not paid the duty.

" 4. A fourth sort, those who buy tea, liquors, linen, handkerchiefs, or anything else
which has not paid duty.

" II. ' But why should they not?   What
harm is there in it ?'

" 1. I answer, open smuggling (such as was

common a few years ago, on the southern coasts especially) is robbing on the highway ; and as much harm as there is in this, just so much there is in smuggling.   A smuggler of this kind is no honester than a highwayman. They may shake hands together.

" 2. Private smuggling is just the same with picking of pockets. There is full as much harm in this as in that. A smuggler of this kind is no honester than a pickpocket. These may shake hands together.

" 3. But open smugglers are worse than common highwaymen, and private smugglers are worse than common pickpockets. For it is undoubtedly worse to rob our father than one we have no obligation to."

This category included the respectable as well as disreputable smugglers.

Notwithstanding his followers were from the ranks of the poorest of the people Mr. Wesley was continually warning them against the dangers of riches.   In his " Thoughts upon Methodism," written August 4, 1786, he says:

" It nearly concerns us to understand how the case stands with us at present.   I fear, wherever riches have increased (exceeding few are the exceptions), the essence of religion, the mind that was in Christ, has decreased in the same proportion.   Therefore do I not see how it is possible, in the nature of things, for any revival of true religion to continue long.   For religion

must necessarily produce both industry and fru-
gality; and these cannot but produce riches.
But as riches increase so will pride, anger, and
love of the world in all its branches.

"How, then, is it possible that Methodism,
that is, the religion of the heart, though it flour-
ishes now as a green bay tree, should continue
in this state? For the Methodists in every
place grow diligent and frugal; consequently,
they increase in goods. Hence, they propor-
tionably increase in pride, in anger, in the desire of the flesh, the desire of the eyes, and the
pride of life. So, although the form of religion
remains, the spirit is swiftly vanishing away.

"Is there no way to prevent this? this continual declension of pure religion? We ought
not to forbid people to be diligent and frugal; we
must exhort all Christians to gain all they can,
and to save all they can; that is, in effect, to
grow rich! What way, then (I ask again), can
we take that our money may not sink us to the
nethermost hell? There is one way, and there
is no other under heaven. If those who 'gain
all they can,' and 'save all they can,' will likewise 'give all they can,' then, the more they
gain the more they will grow in grace, and the
more treasure they will lay up in heaven."

In his sermon on "The Good Steward" Mr.
Wesley, describing the scene when the Lord's
steward is called upon to render his account,
said:

"The Lord of all will next inquire, 'How
3

didst thou employ the worldly goods which I
lodged in thy hands? Didst thou use thy food,
not so as to seek or place thy happiness therein,
but so as to preserve the body in health and
strength and vigor, a fit instrument for the
soul? Didst thou use apparel, not to nourish
pride or vanity, much less to tempt others to
sin, but conveniently and decently to defend thyself from the injuries of the weather? Didst
thou prepare and use thy house, and all other
conveniences, with a single eye to my glory?
In every point seeking not thy own honor, but
mine; studying to please not thyself, but me?'
Once more: 'In what manner didst thou employ
that comprehensive talent, money? Not in
gratifying the desire of the flesh, the desire of
the eye, or the pride of life? Not squandering
it away in vain expenses, the same as throwing
it into the sea? Not hoarding it up to leave
behind thee, the same as burying it in the earth?
But first supplying thy own reasonable wants,
together with those of thy family; then restor-
ing the remainder to me, through the poor,
whom I had appointed to receive it; looking
upon thyself as only one of that number of poor
whose wants were to be supplied out of that
part of my substance which I had placed in thy
hands for this purpose; leaving thee the right of
being supplied first, and the blessedness of giv-
ing rather than receiving? Wast thou accord-
ingly a general benefactor to mankind? Feeding the hungry, clothing the naked, comforting
the sick, assisting the stranger, relieving the

afflicted, according to their various necessities? Wast thou eyes to the blind, and feet to the lame? A father to the fatherless, and a husband to the widow? And didst thou labor to improve all outward works of mercy, as a means of saving souls from death?'"

Whatever may be thought of such admonitions they had great influence upon the members of the societies, very many of whom endeavored by watching and prayer to conform their lives to them, and to help their associates to do likewise. This often required great sacrifice, but Mr. Wesley himself set them a worthy example. He even did more than any others. How he was able to do so much was a mystery to many. He explains in a letter written December 10, 1777:

"You do not at all understand my manner of life. Though I am always in haste I am never in a hurry; because I never undertake any more than I can go through with perfect calmness of spirit. It is true I travel four or five thousand miles in a year. But I generally travel alone in my carriage; and, consequently, am as retired ten hours in a day as if I was in a wilderness. On other days I never spend less than three hours (frequently ten or twelve) in the day alone. So there are few persons in the kingdom who spend so many hours secluded from all company. Yet I find time to visit

the sick and the poor; and I must do it if I
believe the Bible, if I believe these are the marks
whereby the Shepherd of Israel will know and
judge his sheep at the great day; therefore,
when there is time and opportunity for it, who
can doubt but this is a matter of absolute duty?
When I was at Oxford, and lived almost like a
hermit, I saw not how any busy man could be
saved.   I scarce thought it possible for a man
to retain a Christian spirit amid the noise and
bustle of the world.   God taught me better by
my own experience.   I had ten times more
business in America (that is, at intervals) than
ever I had in my life.   But it was no hindrance
to silence of spirit."

The influence of Wesley's teaching and manner of life was not confined to his own followers.   The leaven affected all classes, from the
lowest to the highest.   Says F. W. Farrar,
Dean of Canterbury, in " Prophets of the Christian Faith," published in *The Outlook :*

John Wesley " found a church forgetful and
neglectful of its duties, somnolent in the pleth-
ora of riches, and either unmindful or unwisely
mindful of the poor.   He found churches
empty, dirty, neglected, crumbling into hideous
disrepair; he found the work of the ministry
performed in a manner scandalously perfunc-
tory. . . . But John Wesley, becoming mag-
netic with moral sincerity, flashed into myriads
of hearts fat as brawn, cold as ice, hard as the

nether millstone, the burning spark of his own intense convictions, and thus he saved the Church. . . . It may be that in talent, in imagination, in learning, in the pure and undefinable quality of genius, Wesley was not the equal of many of his contemporaries; but which among them all equaled him in versatility of beneficence, in zeal of self-sacrifice, in the munificence of his generosity, or in the luster of the example he has left to the world? Consider his supreme disinterestedness, his unparalleled courage, his indefatigable toils. How many have there been in all the centuries who made such an absolute offering of his money to God, and, living on less than many a curate's salary, gave away forty thousand pounds? Consider, again, his unparalleled courage. How many have shown equal undauntedness? Men admire the courage of the soldier who heads the forlorn hope through the cross-fire of the batteries, of the sailor or of the fireman who, at personal risk, plucks from destruction an imperiled life; but such physical courage is a million times cheaper and more common than that of the scholar, the gentleman, the clergyman, who, in that age, day after day, month after month, year after year, in England, in America, in Scotland, in Wales, in Ireland, even in the Isle of Man, could, voluntarily and out of the pure love of souls, face raging mobs and descend to what was then regarded as the vulgar humiliation of preaching in the open air. And higher even than this was the moral and spiritual courage which, in the calm of blameless innocence, could treat the most atrocious and the most persistent calumnies with the disdainful indifference of unblemished rectitude. . . .

"Although the world and the Church have learned to be comparatively generous to Wesley, now that a hundred years have sped away, and though the roar of contemporary scandal has long since ceased, I doubt whether even now he is at all adequately appreciated. I doubt whether many are aware of the extent to which to this day the impulse to every great work of philanthropy and social reformation has been due to his energy and insight. The British and Foreign Bible Society, the Religious Tract Society, the London Missionary Society, even the Church Missionary Society, owe not a little to his initiative. The vast spread of religious instruction by weekly periodicals, and the cheap press, with all its stupendous consequences, were inaugurated by him. He gave a great extension to Sunday schools and the work of Robert Raikes. He gave a great impulse both to national education and to technical education, and in starting the work of Silas Told, the Foundry Teacher, he anticipated the humble and holy work of John Pounds, the Portsmouth cobbler. He started in his own person the funeral reform, which is only now beginning to attract public attention, when in his will he directed that at his obsequies there should be no hearse, no escutcheon, no coach, no pomp. He visited prisons and ameliorated the lot of prisoners be-

fore John Howard ; and his very last letter was
written to stimulate William Wilberforce in his
parliamentary labors for the emancipation of the
slave. When we add to this the revival of fervent
worship and devout hymnology among Christian congregations, and their deliverance from
the drawling doggerel of Sternhold and Hop-
kins, and the frigid nullities of Tate and Brady,
we have indeed shown how splendid was the
list of his achievements, and that, as Isaac Tay-
lor says, he furnished ' the starting point for
our modern religious history in all that is char-
acteristic of the present time.'

"And yet, in this long and splendid cata-
logue, we have not mentioned his greatest and
most distinctive work, which was that through
him to the poor the Gospel was again preached.
Let Whitefield have the credit of having been
the first to make the green grass his pulpit and
the heaven his sounding-board ; but Wesley instantly followed, at all costs, the then daring
example, and through all evil report and all
furious opposition he continued it until at last
at Kingswood, at the age of eighty-one, he
preached in the open air, under the shade of
trees which he himself had planted, and sur-
rounded by the children and children's children
of his old disciples, who had long since passed
away. Overwhelming evidence exists to show
what preaching was before and in his day ;
overwhelming evidence exists to show what
the Church and people of England were before and in his day—how dull, how vapid,

how soulless, how Christless was the preaching ; how torpid, how Laodicean was the Church ; how godless, how steeped in immorality was the land. To Wesley was mainly granted the task, for which he was set apart by the hands of invisible consecration—the task which even an archangel might have envied him—of awakening a mighty revival of the religious life in those dead pulpits, in that slumbering Church, in that corrupt society. His was the religious sincerity which not only founded the Wesleyan community, but, working through the heart of the very Church which had despised him, flashed fire into her whitening embers. Changing its outward forms, the work of John Wesley caused, first, the evangelical movement, then the High Church movement, and, in its enthusiasm of humanity, has even reappeared in all that is best in the humble Salvationists, who learned from the example of Wesley what Bishop Lightfoot called 'that lost secret of Christianity, the compulsion of human souls.' Recognizing no utterance of authority as equally supreme with that which came to him from the Sinai of conscience, Wesley did the thing and scorned the consequence. His was the voice which offered hope to the despairing and welcome to the outcast. . . . The poet says :

> " 'Of those three hundred grant but three
> To make a new Thermopylæ.'

And when I think of John Wesley, the organizer, of Charles Wesley, the poet, of George

Whitefield, the orator of this mighty movement, I feel inclined to say of those three self-sacrificing and holy men, Grant but even one to help in the mighty work which yet remains to be accomplished! Had we but three such now,

> " ' Hoary-headed selfishness would feel
> His deathblow, and would totter to his grave ;
> A brighter light attend the human day,
> When every transfer of earth's natural gift
> Should be a commerce of good words and works.'

We have, it is true, hundreds of faithful workers in the Church of England and in other religious communities. But for the slaying of dragons, the rekindlement of irresistible enthusiasm, the redress of intolerable wrongs, a Church needs many Pentecosts and many Resurrections. And these, in the providence of God, are brought about, not by committees and conferences and common workers, but by men who escape the average ; by men who come forth from the multitude ; by men who, not content to trudge on in the beaten paths of commonplace and the cart-ruts of routine, go forth according to their Lord's command, into the highways and hedges ; by men in whom the love of God burns like a consuming flame upon the altar of the heart ; by men who have become electric to make myriads of other souls thrill with their own holy zeal. Such men are necessarily rare, but God's richest boon to any nation, to any society, to any Church is the presence and work of such a man—and such a man was John Wesley."

III.

OPPOSITION TO SLAVERY.

WESLEY'S opposition to human slavery was lifelong and, if the term may be applied to one so full of kindness, bitter. When in Georgia and South Carolina in 1736 he was deeply affected by the heathenish condition of the slaves, but he was unable to do anything for their relief. It is probable, however, that he and the founder of Georgia, Oglethorpe, often talked of the unrighteousness of slavery, and that the determined attitude of Oglethorpe, who declared that the trustees of the colony refused "to make a law permitting such a horrid crime," because "it is against the Gospel as well as against the fundamental law of England," was in part due to Wesley's influence.

The African slave trade was a somewhat respectable business at that date. African slaves had been imported into the United States from the time of Charles V. Las Casas, the famous Spanish missionary, had recommended the first large importation of Negro slaves, to save from destruction by life-destroying overwork his beloved Indians of the West Indies; but, notwithstanding Las Casas afterward bitterly repented his mistake, his Church supported and perpetuated the slave trade and excused the horrors of "the middle passage." During two centuries the Spanish government, " in the name of the Most Holy Trinity," concluded at least ten treaties which authorized the sale of more than five hundred thousand human beings, and received from such traffic a tax of over ten million dollars.

Protestant England was as guilty as Catholic Spain. The first ship which sailed from England, in 1562, to engage in the slave trade bore the sacred name of *Jesus*. For many years English monarchs encouraged the trade, and bishops and clergy approved it. Even Methodism's greatest preacher, "the prince of pulpit orators," George Whitefield, condoned it. His letter to Wesley, written from Georgia, is a most surprising epistle. It must have been a shock to Wesley, even at a time when there were few who denounced the slave trade. This letter reads as follows:

"BRISTOL, *March* 22, 1751.

"REVEREND AND VERY DEAR SIR: Thanks be to God that the time for favoring the colony of Georgia seems to be come. Now is the season for us to exert our utmost for the good of the poor Ethiopians. We are told that even they are soon to stretch out their hands to God; and who knows but their being settled in Georgia may be overruled for this great end? As for the lawfulness of keeping slaves, I have no doubt, since I hear of some that were bought with Abraham's money and some that were born in his house. I also cannot help thinking that some of those servants mentioned by the apostles in their epistles were, or had been, slaves. It is plain that the Gibeonites were doomed to perpetual slavery; and, though liberty is a sweet thing to such as are born free, yet to those who never knew the sweets of it slavery, perhaps, may not be so irksome. However this be, it is plain to a demonstration that hot countries cannot be cultivated without Negroes. What a flourishing country might Georgia have been had the use of them been permitted years ago! How many white people have been destroyed for want of them, and how many thousands of pounds spent to no purpose at all! Though it is true that they are brought in a wrong way from their own country, and it is a trade not to be approved of, yet, as it will be carried on whether we will or not, I should think myself highly favored if I could purchase a good number of them in order to make their lives comfortable, and lay a foundation for breeding up their posterity in the nurture and admonition of the Lord. I had no hand in bringing them into Georgia, though my judgment was for it, and I was

strongly importuned thereto; yet I would not
have a Negro upon my plantation till the use of
them was publicly allowed by the colony.
Now this is done, let us diligently improve the
present opportunity for their instruction.   It
rejoiced my soul to hear that one of my poor
Negroes in Carolina was made a brother in
Christ.   How know we but we may have many
such instances in Georgia!   I trust many of
them will be brought to Jesus, and this consideration, as to us, swallows up all temporal
inconveniences whatsoever.

" I am, etc.,
"GEORGE WHITEFIELD."

Whitefield not only approved of slavery, but
he became a slaveholder, and at the time of his
death possessed seventy-five slaves in connection with his Orphan House plantations in
Georgia.

How early in his career Mr. Wesley began
his open hostility to slavery is not known. His
indirect influence against it began to be exerted
certainly as early as 1758, when a Mr. Gilbert,
of Antigua, Speaker of the House of Assembly,
visiting England in 1758 and 1759, and two of
the four slaves accompanying him were con-
verted in London under Mr. Wesley's preaching.   The converts laid the foundation of the
Wesleyan missions, which did much to prepare
the slaves of the West Indies for emancipation.

Mr. Wesley's first hostile opinion of slavery is found expressed in an entry in his Journal under date of February 12, 1772, in which, contrasting a book he had just read with Sterne's *Sentimental Journey*, which he had read some time before, he writes:

"I read a very different book, published by an honest Quaker, on that execrable sum of all villainies, commonly called the slave trade. I read of nothing like it in the heathen world, ancient or modern; and it infinitely exceeds, in every instance of barbarity, whatever Christian slaves suffer in Mohammedan countries."

Quoting these words, Tyerman says:

"This is a remarkable utterance. It was in this very year that Granville Sharpe, the first of the English antislavery advocates, began to take up the subject; and it was not until fifteen years after this that the Society for the Suppression of the Slave Trade was founded, of which, besides Sharpe, two of the chief members were Thomas Clarkson, a young graduate of Cambridge, and William Wilberforce, who was then Member of Parliament for the county of York. The book which Wesley read was probably written by Anthony Benezet, a French Protestant, who, after being educated in England, became a Quaker in Philadelphia and, in 1762, published the work which first attracted the attention of this country to the inhuman traffic which Wesley so justly

designates 'that execrable sum of all villainies.'
Let it be noted that, besides all his other
honors, John Wesley, the poor, persecuted
Methodist, was one of the first advocates on
behalf of the enthralled African that England
had, and that, sixty years before slavery was
abolished in the dominions of Great Britain, he
denounced the thing in the strongest terms it
was possible to employ."

Mr. Wesley's most powerful contribution to
the antislavery movement was his *Thoughts on
Slavery*. This was an octavo pamphlet of fifty-
three pages, issued in 1774. No more severe
arraignment of slavery than this was ever written. It was sent out in every direction by the
Methodist preachers, and was widely scattered
by them both in Europe and America, and it
probably exerted a greater influence upon the
public conscience than any other book ever
written, not excepting *Uncle Tom's Cabin*, for
the reception of which it prepared the way.
The work met with speedy and vindictive opposition in England, which Wesley expected.
It was soon afterward republished in America
by Mr. Anthony Benezet, of Philadelphia.

The character of the *Thoughts on Slavery* is
indicated by a few extracts. After describing
the method of making war upon native villages
and the capture of natives Mr. Wesley says:

" But in what numbers and in what manner are they carried to America? Mr. Anderson, in his *History of Trade and Commerce*, observes : ' England supplies her American colonies with Negros laves amounting in number to about a hundred thousand every year ;' that is, so many are taken on board our ships, but at least ten thousand of them die in the voyage; about a fourth part more die at the different islands, in what is called the seasoning. So on an average, in the passage and seasoning together, thirty thousand die ; that is, properly, are murdered. O earth, O sea, cover not thou their blood !

" When they are brought down to the shore in order to be sold our surgeons thoroughly examine them, and that quite naked, women and men, without any distinction ; those that are approved are set on one side. In the meantime a burning iron, with the arms or name of the company, lies in the fire, with which they are marked on the breast. Before they are put into the ships their masters strip them of all they have on their backs, so that they come on board stark naked, women as well as men. It is common for several hundred of them to be put on board one vessel, where they are stowed together in as little room as it is possible for them to be crowded. It is easy to suppose what a condition they must soon be in, between heat, thirst, and stench of various kinds. So it is no wonder so many should die in the passage, but rather that any should survive it.

" When the vessels arrive at their destined

port the Negroes are again exposed naked to the eyes of all that flock together, and the examination of their purchasers. Then they are separated to the plantations of their several masters to see each other no more. Here you may see mothers hanging over their daughters, bedewing their naked breasts with tears, and daughters clinging to their parents till the whipper soon obliges them to part. And what can be more wretched than the condition they then enter upon? Banished from their country, from their friends and relations forever, from every comfort of life, they are reduced to a state scarce any way preferable to that of beasts of burden. In general a few roots, not of the nicest kind, usually yams or potatoes, are their food, and two rags that neither screen them from the heat of day nor the cold of the night, their covering. Their sleep is very short, their labor continual and frequently above their strength, so that death sets many of them at liberty before they have lived out half their days. The time they work in the West Indies is from daybreak to noon, and from two o'clock till dark, during which they are attended by overseers, who, if they think them dilatory, or think anything not so well done as it should be, whip them most unmercifully, so that you may see their bodies long after wealed and scarred, usually from the shoulders to the waist. And before they are suffered to go to their quarters they have commonly something to do, as collecting herbage for the horses or gathering fuel

4

for the boilers, so that it is often past twelve
before they can get home. Hence, if their food
is not prepared they are sometimes called to
labor again before they can satisfy their hunger.
And no excuse will avail. If they are not in
the field immediately they must expect to feel
the lash. Did the Creator intend that the noblest creatures in the visible world should live
such a life as this?

"'Are these thy glorious works, Parent of good?'

"As to the punishments inflicted upon them,
says Sir Hans Sloane, 'they frequently geld
them, or chop off half a foot; after they are
whipped till they are raw all over, some put
pepper and salt upon them, some drop melted
wax upon their skin, others cut off their ears,
and constrain them to broil and eat them. For
rebellion—that is, asserting their native liberty,
which they have as much right to as to the air
they breathe—'they fasten them down to the
ground with crooked sticks on every limb, and
then applying fire, by degrees, to the feet and
hands they burn them gradually upward to the
head.'

"But will not the laws made in the plantations prevent or redress all cruelty and oppression? We will take but a few of these laws for
a specimen, and then let any man judge:

"In order to rivet the chain of slavery the
law of Virginia ordains: 'That no slave shall be
set free upon any pretense whatever, except for
some meritorious services to be adjudged and
allowed by the governor and council, and that

where any slave shall be set free by his owner,
otherwise than is herein directed, the church
wardens of the parish wherein such Negro shall
reside for the space of one month are hereby
authorized and required to take up and sell the
said Negro by public outcry.' "

.   .   .   .

Mr. Wesley answers at length the numerous
pleas made in justification of slavery, and in
doing so says:

"That slaveholding is utterly inconsistent
with mercy is almost too plain to need a proof.
Indeed, it is said that, these Negroes being
prisoners of war, our captains and factors buy
them merely to save them from being put to
death. And is not this mercy? I answer,
1. Did Sir John Hawkins, and many others,
seize upon men, women, and children, who were
at peace in their own fields and houses, merely
to save them from death? 2. Was it to save
them from death that they knocked out the
brains of those they could not bring away?
3. Who occasioned and fomented those wars
wherein these poor creatures were taken prisoners? Who excited them by money, by drink,
by every possible means, to fall upon one another? Was it not themselves? They know
in their own conscience it was, if they have any
conscience left. But, 4. To bring the matter
to a short issue, can they say before God that
they ever took a single voyage, or bought a
single Negro, from this motive? They cannot;

they well know, to get money, not to save lives, was the whole and sole spring of their motions.   5. But if this manner of procuring and treating Negroes is not consistent either with mercy or justice, yet there is a plea for it which every man of business will acknowledge to be quite sufficient.   Fifty years ago one meeting an eminent statesman in the lobby of the House of Commons said, 'You have been long talking about justice and equity.   Pray, which is this bill—equity or justice?'   He answered very short and plain, 'D—n justice ; it is necessity.' Here also the slaveholder fixes his feet ; here he rests the strength of his cause.   'If it is not quite right, yet it must be so ; there is an absolute necessity for it.   It is necessary we should procure slaves ; and when we have procured them it is necessary to use them with severity, considering their stupidity, stubbornness, and wickedness.'

"I answer, you stumble at the threshold ; I deny that villainy is ever necessary.   It is impossible that it should ever be necessary for any reasonable creature to violate all the laws of justice, mercy, and truth.   No circumstances can make it necessary for a man to burst in sunder all the ties of humanity.   It can never be necessary for a rational being to sink himself below a brute.   A man can be under no necessity of degrading himself into a wolf.   The absurdity of the supposition is so glaring that one would wonder anyone could help seeing it.

.   .   .   .   .   .

" V. 1. It remains only to make a little application of the preceding observations. But to
whom should that application be made ? That
may bear a question. Should we address ourselves to the public at large ? What effect can
this have ? It may inflame the world against
the guilty, but it is not likely to remove that
guilt. Should we appeal to the English nation
in general? This also is striking wide, and is
never likely to procure any redress for the sore
evil we complain of. As little would it in all
probability avail to apply to the Parliament.
So many things, which seem of greater importance, lie before them, that they are not
likely to attend to this. I therefore add a few
words to those who are more immediately concerned, whether captains, merchants, or planters.

" 2. And, first, to the captains employed in
this trade. Most of you know the country of
Guinea ; several parts of it, at least, between the
river Senegal and the kingdom of Angola.
Perhaps, now, by your means part of it is become a dreary, uncultivated wilderness, the
inhabitants being all murdered or carried away,
so that there are none left to till the ground.
But you well know how populous, how fruitful,
how pleasant it was a few years ago. You
know the people were not stupid, not wanting
in sense, considering the few means of improvement they enjoyed. Neither did you find them
savage, fierce, cruel, treacherous, or unkind to
strangers. On the contrary, they were in most
parts a sensible and ingenious people. They

were kind and friendly, courteous and obliging, and remarkably fair and just in their dealings. Such are the men whom you hire their own countrymen to tear away from this lovely country ; part by stealth, part by force, part made captives in those wars which you raise or foment on purpose. You have seen them torn away—children from their parents, parents from their children, husbands from their wives, wives from their beloved husbands, brethren and sisters from each other. You have dragged them who had never done you any wrong, perhaps in chains, from their native shore. You have forced them into your ships like a herd of swine—them who had souls immortal as your own ; only some of them leaped into the sea, and resolutely stayed under water, till they could suffer no more from you. You have stowed them together as close as ever they could lie, without any regard for decency or convenience. And when many of them had been poisoned by foul air or had sunk under various hardships you have seen their remains delivered to the deep till the sea should give up his dead. You have carried the survivors into the vilest slavery, never to end but with life ; such slavery as is not found among the Turks at Algiers, no, nor among the heathens in America.

" 3. May I speak plainly to you ? I must. Love constrains me ; love to you as well as to those you are concerned with.

" Is there a God ? You know there is. Is he a just God ? Then there must be a state of retribution ; a state wherein the just God will reward every man according to his works. Then what reward will he render to you? O think betimes before you drop into eternity ! Think now, 'He shall have judgment without mercy that showed no mercy.'

"Are you a man ? Then you should have a human heart. But have you, indeed? What is your heart made of? Is there no such principle as compassion there? Do you never feel another's pain? Have you no sympathy, no sense of human woe, no pity for the miserable? When you saw the flowing eyes, the heaving breasts, or the bleeding sides or tortured limbs of your fellow-creatures, was you a stone, or a brute? Did you look upon them with the eyes of a tiger? When you squeezed the agonizing creatures down in the ship, or when you threw their poor mangled remains into the sea, had you no relenting? Did not one tear drop from your eye, one sigh escape from your breast ? Do you feel no relenting now? If you do not you must go on till the measure of your iniquities is full. Then will the great God deal with you as you have dealt with them, and require all their blood at your hands. And at 'that day it shall be more tolerable for Sodom and Gomorrah than for you !' But if your heart does relent, though in a small degree, know it is a call from the God of love. And 'to-day, if you will hear his voice, harden not your heart.' To-day resolve, God being your helper, to escape for your life.

Regard not money! All that a man hath will he give for his life! Whatever you lose, lose not your soul; nothing can countervail that loss. Immediately quit the horrid trade; at all events, be an honest man.

"4. This equally concerns every merchant who is engaged in the slave trade. It is you that induce the African villain to sell his countrymen; and in order thereto to steal, rob, murder men, women, and children without number, by enabling the English villain to pay him for so doing, whom you overpay for his execrable labor. It is your money that is the spring of all, that empowers him to go on; so that whatever he or the African does in this matter is all your act and deed. And is your conscience quite reconciled to this? Does it never reproach you at all? Has gold entirely blinded your eyes and stupefied your heart? Can you see, can you feel, no harm therein? Is it doing as you would be done to? Make the case your own. 'Master,' said a slave at Liverpool to the merchant that owned him,' 'what if some of my countrymen were to come here and take away my mistress, and Master Tommy, and Master Billy, and carry them into our country and make them slaves, how would you like it?' His answer was worthy of a man: 'I will never buy a slave more while I live.' O let his resolution be yours! Have no more part in this detestable business. Instantly leave it to those unfeeling wretches who

'Laugh at human nature and compassion!'

Be you a man, not a wolf, a devourer of the human species! Be merciful that you may obtain mercy!

" 5. And this equally concerns every gentleman that has an estate in our American plantations; yea, all slaveholders, of whatever rank and degree; seeing men-buyers are exactly on a level with men-stealers. Indeed you say, ' I pay honestly for my goods, and I am not concerned to know how they are come by.' Nay, but you are; you are deeply concerned to know they are honestly come by. Otherwise you are a partaker with a thief, and not a jot honester than him. But you know they are not honestly come by; you know they are procured by means nothing near so innocent as picking of pockets, housebreaking, or robbery upon the highway. You know that they are obtained by a deliberate series of more complicated villainy (of fraud, robbery, and murder) than was ever practiced either by Mohammedans or pagans; in particular, by murders of all kinds; by the blood of the innocent poured upon the ground like water. Now, it is your money that pays the merchant, and through him the captain and the African butchers. You therefore are guilty, yea, principally guilty, of all these frauds, robberies, and murders. You are the spring that puts all the rest in motion; they would not stir a step without you; therefore the blood of all these wretches who die before their time, whether in their country or elsewhere, lies on your head.

' The blood of thy brother ' (for, whether thou wilt believe it or no, such he is in the sight of Him that made him) ' crieth against thee from the earth,' from the ship, and from the waters. O, whatever it costs, put a stop to its cry before it be too late; instantly, at any price, were it half of your goods, deliver thyself from bloodguiltiness! Thy hands, thy bed, thy furniture, thy house, thy lands, are at present stained with blood. Surely it is enough; accumulate no more guilt; spill no more the blood of the innocent! Do not hire another to shed blood; do not pay him for doing it! Whether you are a Christian or no, show yourself a man! Be not more savage than a lion or a bear.

" 6. Perhaps you will say, ' I do not buy any Negroes; I only use those left me by my father.' So far it is well; but is it enough to satisfy your own conscience? Had your father, have you, has any man living a right to use another as a slave? It cannot be, even setting revelation aside. It cannot be that either war or contract can give a man such property in another as he has in his sheep and oxen. Much less is it possible that any child of man should ever be born a slave. Liberty is the right of every human creature as soon as he breathes the vital air; and no human law can deprive him of that right which he derives from the law of nature. If, therefore, you have any regard to justice (to say nothing of mercy, nor the revealed law of God), render unto all their due. Give liberty to whom liberty is due, that is, to every child of man, to every partaker of human nature. Let none serve you but by his own act and deed, by his own voluntary choice. Away with all whips, all chains, all compulsion! Be gentle toward all men; and see that you invariably do unto everyone as you would he should do unto you.

" 7. O thou God of love, thou who art loving to every man, and whose mercy is over all thy works; thou who art the Father of the spirits of all flesh, and who art rich in mercy unto all; thou who hast mingled of one blood all the nations upon earth, have compassion on these outcasts of men, who are trodden down as dung upon the earth! Arise, and help those who have no helper, whose blood is spilt upon the ground like water! Are not these also the work of thine own hands, the purchase of thy Son's blood? Stir them to cry to thee in the land of their captivity; and let their complaint come up before thee; let it enter into thy ears! Make even those who lead them away captive to pity them, and to turn their captivity as the rivers in the south. O, burst thou all their chains in sunder; more especially the chains of their sins! Thou Saviour of all, make them free, that they may be free indeed!

> "' The servile progeny of Ham
>   Seize as the purchase of thy blood!
> Let all the heathens know thy name;
>   From idols to the living God
> The dark Americans convert,
>   And shine in every pagan heart!'"

The hostility to slavery expressed in his *Thoughts on Slavery* was manifested by Mr. Wesley to the end. Indeed, the last letter he wrote, four days before his death, was upon this subject. It was addressed to William Wilberforce, leader of the movement for the emancipation of the slaves in the West Indies, and his words were an inspiration to those of his followers in England and America who for many years had been striving to overthrow slavery. His characterization of American slavery as " the vilest that ever saw the sun " was like a bugle blast in arousing his people.

This famous letter is as follows :

" LONDON, *February* 24, 1791.

" DEAR SIR : Unless the divine power has raised you up to be as *Athanasius contra mundum*, I see not how you can go through your glorious enterprise in opposing that execrable villainy which is the scandal of religion, of England, and of human nature. Unless God has raised you up for this very thing, you will be worn out by the opposition of men and devils ; but ' if God be for you, who can be against you ? ' Are all of them stronger than God ? O, ' be not weary in well-doing.' Go on, in the name of God and in the power of his might, till even American slavery, the vilest that ever saw the sun, shall vanish away before it.

" Reading this morning a tract, wrote by a poor African, I was particularly struck by that circumstance—that a man who has a black skin, being wronged or outraged by a white man, can have no redress ; it being a law in all our colonies that the oath of a black against a white goes for nothing.   What villainy is this !

" That He who has guided you from your youth up may continue to strengthen you in this and all things, is the prayer of, dear sir, your affectionate servant,

" JOHN WESLEY."

IV.

INFLUENCE IN AMERICA.

THE missionaries whom Wesley sent to America sympathized with his antislavery views, and early began to preach and talk privately against the hateful system. At the Conference of the preachers in 1780 the following question was asked: "Does this Conference acknowledge that slavery is contrary to the laws of God, man, and nature, and hurtful to society; contrary to the dictates of conscience and pure religion, and doing that which we would not others should do to us and ours? Do we pass our disapprobation on all our friends who keep slaves, and advise their freedom?" The recorded answer to the questions was, "Yes."

The Christmas Conference of 1784, at which the Methodist Episcopal Church was organized, pronounced slavery to be "contrary to the golden law of God . . . and the unalienable right of mankind, as well as every principle of the Revolution."

It took action providing for the emancipation of slaves held by members of the society, and when, six months later, it was "recommended to all our brethren to suspend the execution of the minute on slavery till the deliberations of a future Conference," to this recommendation was added: "N. B.—We do hold in the deepest abhorrence the practice of slavery, and shall not cease to seek its destruction by all wise and prudent means." In the Discipline for 1789 among the General Rules appeared for the first time one respecting slaves. It prohibited "the buying or selling the bodies and souls of men, women, or children with an intention to enslave them."

The first person arrested in America for utterances against slavery was a Methodist preacher, the Rev. Jacob Gruber. Mr. Gruber, who was presiding elder of Carlisle District, in the Baltimore Conference, was invited to preach at a camp meeting held in Washington County, Md., August 16, 1818. He took for his text the words found in Prov. xiv, 34: "Righteousness exalteth a nation; but sin is a reproach to any people." In the course of his remarks he said:

"The last national sin is slavery and oppression. This in particular is a reproach to the nation. Other nations who are under the yoke of despots are pitied, especially when they are ground under the iron heel of oppression. This nation is happily delivered from such bondage. We live in a free country; and that all men are created equal, and have inalienable rights, such as life, liberty, and the pursuit of happiness, we hold as self-evident truths. But there are slaves in our country, and their sweat and blood and tears declare them such. The voice of our brother's blood crieth. Is it not a reproach to a man to hold articles of liberty and independence in one hand and a bloody whip in the other while a Negro stands and trembles before him with his back cut and bleeding?

"There is a laudable zeal manifested in our country to form Bible and missionary societies, to send the Scriptures and the Gospel to heathen nations. Would it not be well for some to be consistent, and instruct the heathens at home in their kitchens, and let them hear the Gospel likewise? What would heathen nations at a distance think if they were told that persons who gave liberally to send them the Bible and the Gospel did not believe, or obey it themselves, or teach their own families to read that book, or allow them time to hear the Gospel of their salvation preached? There is some difference even in this country. We Pennsylvanians think it strange, and it seems quite curious to read in the public prints from some States an advertisement like this: 'For sale, a plantation, a house and lot, horses, cows, sheep, and hogs.

Also, a number of Negroes, men, women, and children, some very valuable ones. Also, a pew in such and such a church.' Again, ' For sale, a likely young Negro, who is an excellent waiter, sold for no fault,' or else ' for want of employment.' These are sold for cash, for four, five, six, seven, or eight hundred dollars a head ; soul and body together, ranked with horses, hogs, etc. Look further and see ' Fifty dollars reward,' ' One hundred dollars reward,' ' Two hundred dollars reward.' What for? Has an apprentice run away from his master ? No ; perhaps a reward for him would be six cents. A man that ran off has probably gone to see his wife, or child, or relations, who have been sold and torn from him, or to enjoy the blessings of a free country and get clear of tyranny. In this inhuman traffic and cruel trade the most tender ties are torn asunder and the nearest connections broken. That which God has joined together let not man put asunder. This solemn injunction is not regarded. Will not God be avenged on such a nation as this ? . . .

"Such alarming and dreadful consequences may attend and follow this reproachful sin in our land and nation :

> " ' Is there not some chosen curse,
> Some secret thunder in the stores of heaven,
> Red with uncommon wrath, to blast the wretch
> That traffics in the blood of souls ? ' "

Some of the slaveholders present were much displeased with the sermon, and a few weeks

5

later a warrant was issued for the arrest of Mr.
Gruber. In the warrant he was charged with
"unlawfully, wickedly, maliciously, and ad-
visedly" endeavoring "to stir up, provoke, in-
stigate, and incite divers Negro slaves . . .
to commit acts of mutiny and rebellion . . .
against the peace, government, and dignity of
the State."

Mr. Gruber was defended by Roger B.
Taney, afterward Chief-Justice of the United
States, and author of the famous Dred-Scott
decision. Mr. Taney in his defense of Mr.
Gruber referred to the well-known attitude of
the Methodist Episcopal Church in regard to
slavery, and uttered these remarkable words:

"It is well known that the gradual and
peaceful abolition of slavery in these States is
one of the objects which the Methodist society
have steadily in view. No slaveholder is allowed to be a minister in that Church. Their
preachers are accustomed, in their sermons, to
speak of the injustice and oppressions of slavery. The opinion of Mr. Gruber on this subject nobody should doubt. And if any slaveholder believed it dangerous to himself, his
family, or the community to suffer his slaves
to learn that all slavery is unjust and oppres-
sive, and persuaded himself that they would not
of themselves be able to make the discovery, it
was in his power to prevent them from attend-

ing the assemblies where such doctrines were likely to be preached. Mr. Gruber did not go to the slaves; they came to him. They could not have come if their masters had chosen to prevent them. . . .

" But the reverend gentleman merits a defense on very different principles. The counsel to whom he had confided his cause cannot content themselves with a cold and reluctant acquittal, and abandon Mr. Gruber, without defense, to all the obloquy and reproach which his enemies have industriously and most unjustly heaped upon him. We cannot consent to buy his safety by yielding to passion, prejudice, and avarice, the control of future discussions on this great and important question. He must not surrender up the civil and religious rights secured to him, in common with others, by the Constitution of this most favored nation. Mr. Gruber feels that it is due to his own character, to the station he fills, to the respectable society of Christians in which he is a minister of the Gospel, not only to defend himself from this prosecution, but also to avow, and to vindicate here, the principles he maintained in his sermon. There is no law that forbids us to speak of slavery as we think of it. Any man has a right to publish his opinions on that subject whenever he pleases. It is a subject of national concern, and may at all times be freely discussed. Mr. Gruber did quote the language of our great act of national independence, and insisted on the principles

contained in that venerated instrument. He
did rebuke those masters who, in the exercise of
power, are deaf to the calls of humanity; and
he warned them of the evils they might bring
upon themselves. He did speak with abhorrence of those reptiles who live by trading in
human flesh and enrich themselves by tearing
the husband from the wife, the infant from
the bosom of the mother; and this, I am instructed, was the head and front of his offend-
ing. Shall I content myself with saying he
had a right to say this? that there is no
law to punish him? So far is he from being
the object of punishment in any form of pro-
ceeding that we are prepared to maintain the
same principles, and to use, if necessary, the
same language here in the temple of justice,
and in the presence of those who are the ministers of the law.

"A hard necessity, indeed, compels us to
endure the evil of slavery for a time. It was
imposed upon us by another nation, while we
were yet in a state of colonial vassalage. It
cannot be easily or suddenly removed. Yet,
while it continues, it is a blot on our national
character, and every real lover of freedom con-
fidently hopes that it will be effectually, though
it must be gradually, wiped away, and earnestly looks for the means by which this necessary object may be best attained. And until
it shall be accomplished, until the time shall
come when we can point without a blush to
the language held in the Declaration of Inde-

pendence, every friend of humanity will seek to lighten the galling chain of slavery, and better, to the utmost of his power, the wretched condition of the slave."

Mr. Gruber was acquitted.

Not all followers of Mr. Wesley in America accepted his antislavery views. Even the General Conference for a time receded from the high position taken by the Conference of 1784, and leading ministers in the Church sought by Conference action and official authority to silence the opponents of slavery. One Annual Conference in 1838 declared that, "*Whereas*, there is a clause in the Discipline of our Church which states that we are as much as ever convinced of the great evil of slavery; and *whereas*, the said clause has been perverted by some and used in such a manner as to produce the impression that the Methodist Episcopal Church believed slavery to be a moral evil; therefore, *resolved*, that it is the sense of the Georgia Annual Conference that slavery, as it exists in the United States, is not a moral evil."

Notwithstanding the divided opinions of his followers, John Wesley's words, especially his declaration that " American slavery [was] the vilest that ever saw the sun," continued their work of molding public opinion and were a large factor in the division of the Church in 1844, which action contributed largely to the growth of the sentiment against slavery and to its final overthrow.

V.

A FRUITFUL SERMON.

ONE of the most notable of Wesley's sermons, and in many respects one of the most fruitful in its influence upon the dress and practices of early Methodists in England and America, was that on "The Use of Money." Many thousands patterned their lives by its instructions. It would not be wise, perhaps, to practice some of its precepts to-day, under conditions very different from those existing when the sermon was delivered, but for the most part its spirit and lessons are as applicable as they were in England a century and more ago. Christians of the present time, whether they be rich or poor, may well accept it as a message from one of Jehovah's prophets, and adapt it to their own needs. The sermon is as follows:

THE USE OF MONEY.

"I say unto you, Make to yourselves friends of the mammon of unrighteousness; that, when ye fail, they may receive you into everlasting habitations."—Luke xvi, 9.

1. Our Lord, having finished the beautiful parable of the prodigal son, which he had particularly addressed to those who murmured at

his receiving publicans and sinners, adds another relation of a different kind, addressed
rather to the children of God. " He said unto
his disciples "—not so much to the scribes and
Pharisees, to whom he had been speaking before—" There was a certain rich man, who had a
steward, and he was accused to him of wasting
his goods. . And calling him, he said, Give
an account of thy stewardship; for thou canst
be no longer steward " (verses 1, 2). After re-
citing the method which the bad steward used
to provide against the day of necessity our
Saviour adds, " His lord commended the unjust
steward," namely, in this respect, that he used
timely precaution; and subjoins this weighty
reflection, " The children of this world are
wiser in their generation than the children of
light " (verse 8); those who seek no other portion than this wòrld "are wiser " (not absolutely; for they are, one and all, the veri-
est fools, the most egregious madmen under
heaven; but, "in their generation," in their
own way; they are more consistent with themselves; they are truer to their acknowledged
principles; they more steadily pursue their
end) "than the children of light "—than they
who see " the light of the glory of God in the
face of Jesus Christ." Then follow the words
above recited : "And I "—the only begotten
Son of God, the Creator, Lord, and Possessor
of heaven and earth and all that is therein; the
Judge of all, to whom ye are to "give an account of your stewardship," when ye " can be

no longer stewards;" "I say unto you"—
learn in this respect, even of the unjust steward
—"make yourselves friends," by wise, timely
precaution, "of the mammon of unrighteousness." "Mammon" means riches, or money.
It is termed "the mammon of unrighteousness" because of the unrighteous manner
wherein it is frequently procured, and wherein
even that which was honestly procured is generally employed. "Make yourselves friends"
of this, by doing all possible good, particularly to the children of God; "that when
ye fail"—when ye return to dust, when ye
have no more place under the sun—those of
them who are gone before "may receive you,"
may welcome you, into "everlasting habitations."

2. An excellent branch of Christian wisdom
is here inculcated by our Lord on all his followers, namely, the right use of money; a subject
largely spoken of, after their manner, by men
of the world, but not sufficiently considered by
those whom God hath chosen out of the world.
These, generally, do not consider, as the importance of the subject requires, the use of this
excellent talent. Neither do they understand
how to employ it to the greatest advantage;
the introduction of which into the world is one
admirable instance of the wise and gracious
providence of God. It has, indeed, been the
manner of poets, orators, and philosophers, in
almost all ages and nations, to rail at this as
the grand corrupter of the world, the bane of

virtue, the pest of human society. Hence, nothing so commonly heard as,

> "*Ferrum, ferroque nocentius aurum,*"
> "And gold, more mischievous than keenest steel."

Hence the lamentable complaint,

> "*Effodiuntur opes, irritamenta malorum,*"
> "Wealth is dug up, incentive to all ill."

Nay, one celebrated writer gravely exhorts his countrymen, in order to banish all vice at once, to " throw all their money into the sea: "

> "*In mare proximum,*
> *Summi materiem mali!*"

But is not all this mere empty rant? Is there any solid reason therein? By no means. For, let the world be as corrupt as it will, is gold or silver to blame? "The love of money," we know, " is the root of all evil;" but not the thing itself. The fault does not lie in the money, but in them that use it. It may be used ill; and what may not? But it may like-wise be used well; it is full as applicable to the best as to the worst uses. It is of unspeak-able service to all civilized nations, in all the common affairs of life; it is a most compendi-ous instrument of transacting all manner of business, and (if we use it according to Chris-tian wisdom) of doing all manner of good. It is true, were man in a state of innocence, or were all men 'filled with the Holy Ghost," so that, like the infant Church at Jerusalem, " no man counted anything he had his own," but " distribution was made to everyone as he had need," the use of it would be superseded, as we cannot conceive there is anything of the kind among the inhabitants of heaven. But, in the present state of mankind, it is an excellent gift of God, answering the noblest ends. In the hands of his children it is food for the hungry, drink for the thirsty, raiment for the naked; it gives to the traveler and the stranger where to lay his head. By it we may supply the place of a husband to the widow and of a father to the fatherless. We may be a defense for the oppressed, a means of health to the sick, of ease to them that are in pain; it may be as eyes to the blind, as feet to the lame; yea, a lifter up from the gates of death!

3. It is, therefore, of the highest concern that all who fear God know how to employ this valuable talent; that they be instructed how it may answer these glorious ends, and in the highest degree. And perhaps all the instructions which are necessary for this may be reduced to three plain rules, by the exact observance whereof we may approve ourselves faithful stewards of "the mammon of unrighteousness."

I. 1. The first of these is (he that heareth, let him understand!), "Gain all you can." Here we may speak like the children of the world; we meet them on their own ground. And it is our bounden duty to do this; we ought to gain all we can gain, without buying gold too dear, without paying more for it than it is worth. But this it is certain we ought not to do: we ought not to gain money at the expense of life, nor (which is in effect the same thing) at the expense of our health. Therefore no gain whatsoever should induce us to enter into, or to continue in, any employ which is of such a kind or is attended with so hard or so long labor as to impair our constitution. Neither should we begin or continue in any business which necessarily deprives us of proper seasons for food and sleep in such a proportion as our nature requires. Indeed, there is a great difference here. Some employments are absolutely and totally unhealthy, as those which imply the dealing much with arsenic or other equally hurtful minerals, or the breathing an air tainted with steams of melting lead, which must at length destroy the firmest constitution. Others may not be absolutely unhealthy, but only to persons of a weak constitution. Such are those which require many hours to be spent in writing; especially if a person write sitting, and lean upon the stomach, or remain long in an uneasy posture. But whatever it is which reason or experience shows to be destructive of health or strength, that we may not submit to; seeing "the life is more [valuable] than meat, and the body than raiment;" and if we are already engaged in such an employ we should exchange it, as soon as possible, for some which, if it lessen our gain, will, however, not lessen our health.

2. We are, secondly, to gain all we can without hurting our mind, any more than our body.

For neither may we hurt this; we must preserve, at all events, the spirit of a healthful
mind. Therefore we may not engage or continue in any sinful trade, any that is contrary
to the law of God or of our country. Such are
all that necessarily imply our robbing or de-
frauding the king of his lawful customs. For
it is at least as sinful to defraud the king of his
right as to rob our fellow-subjects; and the
king has full as much right to his customs as
we have to our houses and apparel. Other
businesses there are which, however innocent
in themselves, cannot be followed with innocence now, at least not in England: such, for
instance, as will not afford a competent main-
tenance without cheating or lying or conform-
ity to some custom which is not consistent with
a good conscience: these, likewise, are sacredly
to be avoided, whatever gain they may be attended with, provided we follow the custom of
the trade; for, to gain money, we must not
lose our souls. There are yet others which we
may pursue with perfect innocence, without
hurting either body or mind, and yet perhaps
you cannot; either they may entangle you in
that company which would destroy your soul,
and by repeated experiments it may appear
that you cannot separate the one from the
other, or there may be an idiosyncrasy, a pecul-
iarity in your constitution of soul (as there is
in the bodily constitution of many), by reason
whereof that employment is deadly to you
which another may safely follow. So I am

convinced, from many experiments, I could not study to any degree of perfection either mathematics, arithmetic, or algebra without being a deist, if not an atheist; and yet others may study them all their lives without sustaining any inconvenience. None, therefore, can here determine for another; but every man must judge for himself, and abstain from whatever he, in particular, finds to be hurtful to his soul.

3. We are, thirdly, to gain all we can without hurting our neighbor. But this we may not, cannot do, if we love our neighbor as ourselves. We cannot, if we love everyone as ourselves, hurt anyone *in his substance*. We cannot devour the increase of his lands, and perhaps the lands and houses themselves by gaming, by overgrown bills (whether on account of physic, of law, or anything else), or by requiring or taking such interest as even the laws of our country forbid. Hereby all pawnbroking is excluded; seeing whatever good we might do thereby all unprejudiced men see with grief to be abundantly overbalanced by the evil. And if it were otherwise, yet we are not allowed to "do evil that good may come." We cannot, consistent with brotherly love, sell our goods below the market price; we cannot study to ruin our neighbor's trade in order to advance our own; much less can we entice away, or receive, any of his servants or workmen whom he has need of. None can gain by swallowing up his neighbor's substance without gaining the damnation of hell!

4. Neither may we gain by hurting our neighbor *in his body*. Therefore we may not sell anything which tends to impair health. Such is, eminently, all that liquid fire commonly called drams, or spirituous liquors. It is true, these may have a place in medicine; they may be of use in some bodily disorders; although there would rarely be occasion for them were it not for the unskillfulness of the practitioner. Therefore such as prepare and sell them only for this end may keep their conscience clear. But who are they? Who prepare them only for this end? Do you know ten such distillers in England? Then excuse these. But all who sell them in the common way, to any that will buy, are poisoners general. They murder his majesty's subjects by wholesale; neither does their eye pity or spare. They drive them to hell like sheep; and what is their gain? Is it not the blood of these men? Who then wou'd envy their large estates and sumptuous palaces? A curse is in the midst of them; the curse of God cleaves to the stones, the timber, the furniture of them! The curse of God is in their gardens, their walks, their groves; a fire that burns to the nethermost hell! Blood, blood is there; the foundation, the floor, the walls, the roof, are stained with blood! And canst thou hope, O, thou man of blood, though thou art "clothed in scarlet and fine linen, and farest sumptuously every day," canst thou hope to deliver down thy *fields of blood* to the third generation? Not so; for there is a God in

heaven ; therefore thy name shall soon be rooted out.   Like as those whom thou hast destroyed, body and soul, " thy memorials shall perish with thee ! "

5. And are not they partakers of the same guilt, though in a lower degree, whether surgeons, apothecaries, or physicians, who play with the lives or health of men, to enlarge their own gain ? who purposely lengthen the pain or disease which they are able to remove speedily ? who protract the cure of their patient's body in order to plunder his substance ? Can any man be clear before God who does not shorten every disorder " as much as he can," and remove all sickness and pain " as soon as he can ? "   He cannot ; for nothing can be more clear than that he does not " do unto others as he would they should do unto himself."

6. This is dear-bought gain.   And so is whatever is procured by hurting our neighbor *in his soul ;* by ministering, suppose, either directly or indirectly, to his unchastity or intemperance, which certainly none can do who has any fear of God or any real desire of pleasing him.   It nearly concerns all those to consider this who have anything to do with taverns, victualing houses, opera houses, play houses, or any other places of public fashionable diversion.   If these profit the souls of men you are clear ; your employment is good and your gain innocent ; but if they are either sinful in themselves or natural inlets to sin of various kinds, then, it is to be feared, you have a sad account to make.   O,

beware lest God say in that day, " These have perished in their iniquity, but their blood do I require at thy hands!"

7. These cautions and restrictions being observed, it is the bounden duty of all who are engaged in worldly business to observe that first and great rule of Christian wisdom with respect to money, "Gain all you can." Gain all you can by honest industry. Use all possible diligence in your calling. Lose no time. If you understand yourself and your relation to God and man you know you have none to spare. If you understand your particular calling, as you ought, you will have no time that hangs upon your hands. Every business will afford some employment sufficient for every day and every hour. That wherein you are placed, if you follow it in earnest, will leave you no leisure for silly, unprofitable diversions. You have always something better to do, something that will profit you more or less. And " whatsoever thy hand findeth to do, do it with thy might." Do it as soon as possible ; no delay! no putting off from day to day or from hour to hour. Never leave anything till to-morrow which you can do to-day. And do it as well as possible. Do not sleep or yawn over it ; put your whole strength to the work. Spare no pains. Let nothing be done by halves or in a slight and careless manner. Let nothing in your business be left undone if it can be done by labor or patience.

8. Gain all you can by common sense, by

6

using in your business all the understanding which God has given you. It is amazing to observe how few do this; how men run on in the same dull track with their forefathers. But, whatever they do who know not God, this is no rule for you. It is a shame for a Christian not to improve upon *them*, in whatever he takes in hand. You should be continually learning, from the experience of others or from your own experience, reading and reflection, to do everything you have to do better to-day than you did yesterday. And see that you practice whatever you learn, that you may make the best of all that is in your hands.

II. 1. Having gained all you can, by honest wisdom and unwearied diligence, the second rule of Christian prudence is, "Save all you can." Do not throw the precious talent into the sea : leave that folly to heathen philosophers. Do not throw it away in idle expenses, which is just the same as throwing it into the sea. Expend no part of it merely to gratify the desire of the flesh, the desire of the eye, or the pride of life.

2. Do not waste any part of so precious a talent merely in gratifying the desires of the flesh ; in procuring the pleasures of sense of whatever kind ; particularly in enlarging the pleasure of tasting. I do not mean avoid gluttony and drunkenness only ; an honest heathen would condemn these. But there is a regular, reputable kind of sensuality, an elegant epicurism, which does not immediately disorder the stom-

ach, nor (sensibly at least) impair the understanding ; and yet (to mention no other effects of it now) it cannot be maintained without considerable expense. Cut off all this expense. Despise delicacy and variety, and be content with what plain nature requires.

3. Do not waste any part of so precious a talent merely in gratifying the desire of the eye, by superfluous or expensive apparel, or by needless ornaments. Waste no part of it in curiously adorning your houses ; in superfluous or expensive furniture ; in costly pictures, painting, gilding, books ; in elegant rather than useful gardens. Let your neighbors who know nothing better do this. " Let the dead bury their dead." But "what is that to thee?" says our Lord. " Follow thou me." Are you willing? Then you are able so to do !

4. Lay out nothing to gratify the pride of life ; to gain the admiration or praise of men. This motive of expense is frequently interwoven with one or both of the former. Men are expensive in diet, or apparel, or furniture, not barely to please their appetite, or to gratify their eye, or their imagination, but their vanity too. " So long as thou doest well unto thyself men will speak good of thee." So long as thou art " clothed in purple and fine linen, and farest sumptuously every day," no doubt many will applaud thy elegance of taste, thy generosity and hospitality. But do not buy their applause so dear. Rather be content with the honor that cometh from God.

5. Who would expend anything in gratifying these desires if he considered that to gratify them is to increase them? Nothing can be more certain than this: daily experience shows the more they are indulged they increase the more. Whenever, therefore, you expend anything to please your taste or other senses you pay so much for sensuality. When you lay out money to please your eye you give so much for an increase of curiosity—for a stronger attachment to these pleasures which perish in the using. While you are purchasing anything which men use to applaud you are purchasing more vanity. Had you not then enough of vanity, sensuality, curiosity, before? Was there need of any addition? And would you pay for it too? What manner of wisdom is this? Would not the literally throwing your money into the sea be a less mischievous folly?

6. And why should you throw away money upon your children any more than upon yourself, in delicate food, in gay or costly apparel, in superfluities of any kind? Why should you purchase for them more pride or lust, more vanity or foolish and hurtful desires? They do not want any more; they have enough already; nature has made ample provision for them; why should you be at farther expense to increase their temptations and snares and to pierce them through with many sorrows?

7. Do not leave it to them to throw away. If you have good reason to believe they would waste what is now in your possession, in grati-

fying, and thereby increasing, the desire of the flesh, the desire of the eye, or the pride of life, at the peril of theirs and your own soul, do not set these traps in their way. Do not offer your sons or your daughters unto Belial any more than unto Moloch. Have pity upon them, and remove out of their way what you may easily foresee would increase their sins, and consequently plunge them deeper into ever-lasting perdition! How amazing, then, is the infatuation of those parents who think they can never leave their children enough! What! cannot you leave them enough of arrows, fire-brands, and death? Not enough of foolish and hurtful desires? Not enough of pride, lust, ambition, vanity? Not enough of everlasting burnings? Poor wretch! Thou fearest where no fear is. Surely both thou and they, when ye are lifting up your eyes in hell, will have enough both of " the worm that never dieth " and of " the fire that never shall be quenched! "

8. " What then would you do if you were in my case—if you had a considerable fortune to leave ? " Whether I *would* do it or no, I know what I *ought* to do ; this will admit of no reasonable question. If I had one child, elder or younger, who knew the value of money, one who I believed would put it to the true use, I should think it my absolute, indispensable duty to leave that child the bulk of my fortune, and to the rest just so much as would enable them to live in the manner they had been accus-tomed to do. " But what if all your children

were equally ignorant of the true use of money?" I ought then (hard saying! who can hear it?) to give each what would keep him above want, and to bestow all the rest in such a manner as I judged would be most for the glory of God.

III. 1. But let not any man imagine that he has done anything barely by going thus far, by " gaining and saving all he can," if he were to stop here. All this is nothing if a man go not forward, if he does not point all this at a farther end. Nor, indeed, can a man properly be said to save anything if he only lays it up. You may as well throw your money into the sea as bury it in the earth. And you may as well bury it in the earth as in your chest or in the Bank of England. Not to use is effectually to throw it away. If, therefore, you would indeed " make yourselves friends of the mammon of unrighteousness," add the third rule to the two preceding. Having first gained all you can, and, secondly, saved all you can, then " give all you can."

2. In order to see the ground and reason of this, consider, when the Possessor of heaven and earth brought you into being, and placed you in this world, he placed you here, not as a proprietor, but a steward; as such he intrusted you for a season with goods of various kinds, but the sole property of these still rests in him, nor can ever be alienated from him. As you yourself are not your own, but his, such is, likewise, all that you enjoy. Such is your soul and your

body, not your own, but God's. And so is your substance, in particular. And he has told you in the most clear and express terms how you are to employ it for him, in such a manner that it may be all a holy sacrifice, acceptable through Christ Jesus. And this light, easy service he hath promised to reward with an eternal weight of glory.

3. The directions which God has given us touching the use of our worldly substance may be comprised in the following particulars. If you desire to be a faithful and a wise steward, out of that portion of your Lord's goods which he has for the present lodged in your hands, but with the right of resuming whenever it pleases him, first, provide things needful for yourself, food to eat, raiment to put on, whatever nature moderately requires for preserving the body in health and strength. Secondly, provide these for your wife, your children, your servants, or any others who pertain to your household. If, when this is done, there be an overplus left, then " do good to them that are of the household of faith." If there be an overplus still, "as you have opportunity, do good unto all men." In so doing you give all you can ; nay, in a sound sense, all you have ; for all that is laid out in this manner is really given to God. You " render unto God the things that are God's," not only by what you give to the poor, but also by that which you expend in providing things needful for yourself and your household.

4. If then a doubt should at any time arise in your mind concerning what you are going to expend, either on yourself, or any part of your family, you have an easy way to remove it. Calmly and seriously inquire, 1. In expending this am I acting according to my character? Am I acting herein, not as a proprietor, but as a steward of my Lord's goods? 2. Am I doing this in obedience to his word? In what Scripture does he require me so to do? 3. Can I offer up this action, this expense as a sacrifice to God through Jesus Christ? 4. Have I reason to believe that for this very work I shall have a reward at the resurrection of the just? You will seldom need anything more to remove any doubt which arises on this head; but by this fourfold consideration you will receive clear light as to the way wherein you should go.

5. If any doubt still remain you may farther examine yourself by prayer, according to those heads of inquiry. Try whether you can say to the Searcher of hearts, your conscience not condemning you, " Lord, thou seest I am going to expend this sum on that food, apparel, furniture. And thou knowest I act therein with a single eye, as a steward of thy goods, expending this portion of them thus, in pursuance of the design thou hast in intrusting me with them. Thou knowest I do this in obedience to thy word, as thou commandest, and because thou commandest it. Let this, I beseech thee, be a holy sacrifice, acceptable

through Jesus Christ! And give me a witness in myself that for this labor of love I shall have a recompense when thou rewardest every man according to his works." Now if your conscience bear you witness in the Holy Ghost that this prayer is well-pleasing to God, then have you no reason to doubt but that expense is right and good, and such as will never make you ashamed.

6. You see, then, what it is to "make yourselves friends of the mammon of unrighteousness," and by what means you may procure "that when ye fail they may receive you into everlasting habitations." You see the nature and extent of truly Christian prudence so far as it relates to the use of that great talent, money. Gain all you can without hurting either yourself or your neighbor, in soul or body, by applying hereto with unintermitted diligence and with all the understanding which God has given pou; save all you can by cutting off every expense which serves only to indulge foolish desire to gratify either the desire of the flesh, the desire of the eye, or the pride of life; waste nothing, living or dying, on sin or folly, whether for yourself or your children; and then give all you can, or, in other words, give all you have, to God. Do not stint yourself, like a Jew rather than a Christian, to this or that proportion. Render unto God, not a tenth, not a third, not half, but all that is God's, be it more or less, by employing all, on yourself, your household, the household of faith, and all mankind, in such a

manner that you may give a good account of
your stewardship, when ye can be no longer
stewards ; in such a manner as the oracles of
God direct, both by general and particular precepts; in such a manner that whatever ye do
may be " a sacrifice of a sweet-smelling savor
to God," and that every act may be rewarded
in that day when the Lord cometh with all his
saints.

7. Brethren, can we be either wise or faithful stewards unless we thus manage our Lord's
goods ? We cannot, as not only the oracles of
God, but our own conscience, beareth witness.
Then why should we delay ? Why should
we confer any longer with flesh and blood, or
men of the world? Our kingdom, our wisdom,
is not of this world ; heathen custom is nothing
to us. We follow no men any farther than
they are followers of Christ. Hear ye him ;
yea, to-day, while it is called to-day, hear and
obey his voice ! At this hour, and from this
hour, do his will ; fulfill his word in this and in
all things ! I entreat you, in the name of the
Lord Jesus, act up to the dignity of your calling ! No more sloth ! Whatsoever your hand
findeth to do, do it with your might ! No
more waste ! Cut off every expense which
fashion, caprice, or flesh and blood demand.
No more covetousness ! But employ whatever
God has intrusted you with in doing good, all
possible good, in every possible kind and degree, to the household of faith, to all men !
This is no small part of " the wisdom of the

just." Give all ye have, as well as all ye are, a spiritual sacrifice to Him who withheld not from you his Son, his only Son ; so "laying up in store for yourselves a good foundation against. the time to come, that ye may attain eternal life."

VI.

Influence upon the Labor Movement.

THE moral condition of England at the beginning of the Methodist movement is thus described by Mr. Wesley in his *Appeal to Men of Reason and Religion*, published in 1745:

"What can an impartial person think concerning the present state of religion in England? Is there a nation under the sun which is so deeply fallen from the very first principles of all religion? Where is the country in which is found so utter a disregard to even heathen morality; such a thorough contempt of justice and truth and all that should be dear and honorable to rational creatures?

"What species of vice can possibly be named, even of those that nature itself abhors, of which we have not had for many years a plentiful and still increasing harvest? What sin remains, either in Rome or Constantinople, which we have not imported long ago (if it was not of our native growth), and improved upon ever since? Such a complication of villainies of every kind, considered with all their aggravations; such a scorn of whatever bears the face of virtue; such injustice, fraud, and falsehood; above all, such perjury and such a method of law, we may defy the whole world to produc."

Equally deplorable was the industrial condition of the people then, and for many years afterward. That of the miners and agricultural laborers, or peasants, as they were called, was particularly bad.

"The generality of English peasants," wrote Mr. Wesley in 1756, "are not only grossly, stupidly, I had almost said brutishly, ignorant as to all the arts of this life, but eminently so with regard to religion and the life to come.   Ask a countryman, 'What is faith? What is repentance? What is holiness? What is true religion?' and he is no more able to give you an intelligible answer than if you were to ask him about the Northeast Passage.   Is there, then, any possibility that they should practice what they know nothing of?   If religion is not even in their heads can it be in their hearts or lives? It cannot.   Nor is there the least savor thereof either in their tempers or conversation.   Neither in the one nor the other do they rise one jot above the pitch of a Turk or a heathen."

But wretched as was the lot of the peasant it was much better than the terrible toil and hardship of the miner and the factory worker. Until the nineteenth century was far advanced thousands of children from four to five years of age worked as trappers amid the darkness and the horrors of the pit, and never saw the sunshine except on Sundays.   Women were employed as beasts of burden, and with chains around their waists crawled on hands and knees through narrow passages, drawing after them the coal carriages. Girls and women carried on their backs burdens often weighing a hundred and fifty pounds, and little children of six and seven years of age carried coal creels weighing fifty pounds up stairs that, in the aggregate, equaled an ascent fourteen times a day to the summit of St. Paul's Cathedral. Other children were daily required to work for thirteen and fourteen hours pumping water from the mine ; and it is stated that they would "often be standing for thirty-six hours ankle-deep in the water." Their pay was a mere pittance, and they were obliged to spend that at the "truck stores," where they were charged twenty-five per cent more for everything they bought than they would have paid elsewhere. Men were also required to work thirteen or fourteen hours ; they were the victims of injustice and oppression ; rheumatism was universal and consumption common. Deaths from accident were of almost daily occurrence. But there has been a marked improvement in the condition of the miner, and he has himself become a leader in the movement for bettering the condition of all classes of working people.

"The miner," says Mr. T. R. Threlfall, Secretary of the Labor Electoral Association, "is a strong personality in the industrial world.   He is the pioneer of the labor movement. Possessing the physical vigor of the agricultural laborer, the astuteness of the town artisan, and that desire for knowledge which is the keynote to progress, he has learned amid the dark passages in the mine, while the shadow of death hovered over him, to understand somewhat the solemnity of life, to be awed by the infinite, and in many cases to find solace in religion. He turned to Methodism, and found therein a faith in keeping with his sturdy, hopeful nature. The miner's attachment to Methodism is of long standing.   It dates from the time when Wesley discoursed to the pitmen of Northumberland and Durham, who received him with open arms.   Here the faith found congenial soil, for it was planted amid a people traditionally religious, whose ancestors had lived for centuries beneath the shadow of the monastery, and who had been faithful to their ancient Church when king and Parliament assailed it. The relics of St. Cuthbert were a charm in the forests and morasses lying between the Tyne and the Wear and over the wild borderlands of Northumberland.   And when at length this stately Church was stripped of its power and glory, its abbeys overthrown and its priests dispersed, these Northern men did not take kindly to its successors, but spiritually slumbered until the Wesleys broke the spell.   Since then

Methodism has become the dominant faith of the miners. Such affinity of the vanguard of labor for this particular Church is not only eloquent for the past but is significant for the future. It is not based upon local peculiarities, upon conditions of employment, upon tradition or material surroundings, but springs from the fact that Methodism has nearly approached the miner's conception of a democratic Church. Its spiritual zeal aroused him, its democratic instincts were in keeping with his political aspirations, and its organizing ability educated him in the principles of unity."

With the conversion of their souls many of the miners seemed to receive the gift of tongues, and not only the power to tell of the experience of salvation in their hearts and to appeal to their fellow-workers to give up their sins, but a consciousness of the social and industrial wrongs of which they were the victims, and the moral courage to protest against them and to seek deliverance. Soon they began to organize, and their spiritual leaders, the Methodist local preachers, became their industrial leaders. Mr. Threlfall, in an article on "The Faith of the Miners," in the *London Methodist Times*, in 1890, wrote as follows:

"Methodism has undoubtedly played a very important part in organizing miners. No one can read the detailed history of the great strikes in the mining world without observing how many of the leaders are connected with some branch of the Methodist Church. Take the first great Northumberland strike in 1831 as an instance. Name after name of those who organized it, guided it, and were imprisoned for it are those of local preachers. Nor was this feature confined to Northumberland and Durham ; it is a feature of all the mining struggles in Yorkshire and Wales, in Cornwall and Derbyshire. But these men had learned other things from their connection with Methodism than training as speakers. They had obtained education in the art of organization, and this they put to good use. The result is that to-day no workmen are so well organized as the miners, none have more nearly approached a national federation, and none have been so quick to perceive the utility of direct representation in Parliament. Can there be any more striking tribute to the influence of Methodism upon the mining community than the fact that the five miners' members in the House of Commons have all been trained in the Methodist Church, four being past or present local preachers? In the Parliament of 1885 there were six, the last one being Mr. John Wilson, C.C., ex-M. P. for Houghton-le-Spring, treasurer of the Durham Miners' Association, and the president of the Labor Electoral Association.

" Nor is this the only evidence of the militant force of Methodism in the democratic movement. While I write there lies before me an

extensive list of miners' leaders who either have
been, or are now, local preachers.   The Northumberland and Durham miners are, of course,
well represented; next comes the Yorkshire
Miners' Association, with three of the leading
officials and a host of branch leaders; one of
the two agents of the Derbyshire Miners; the
agents of the Forest of Dean miners, and the
Notts miners; and a long array of names well
known in the mining world.   Lancashire, Staf-
fordshire, the Midlands, Notts, Derbyshire, and
other coal fields, all furnish a considerable number.   Indeed, looking at this list, and compar-
ing it with the names of delegates attending
the great miners' conferences, when from three
hundred thousand to four hundred thousand
men are occasionally represented, it is no ex-
aggeration to say that fully one half served an
apprenticeship as local preachers."

When in 1874 the miners decided that labor
should be represented in Parliament by one of
their own order they selected as their repre-
sentative Thomas Burt.   He was elected by a
majority of three thousand in a constituency of
four thousand, and has represented labor in
Parliament ever since.   Mr. Burt has been president of the Miners' International Union, and
was the English delegate to the Berlin Labor
Congress called by the Emperor of Germany.
Of Mr. Burt, a writer in an English paper some
months ago said:

" Mr. Burt, the miner, who sits in Parliament for Morpeth, and who possesses the distinction of having sat there since 1874 without having lost those good qualities which led his fellow-miners to elect him, is also a Methodist. He was, as our readers already know, one of the British delegates attending the International Labor Conference, which was presided over by the German emperor. Mr. Burt had a pleasant little conversation with the emperor at one of the state receptions at the imperial palace. It must have been an interesting sight—the head of the German empire chatting with the quiet, unassuming Methodist miner-member of the English House of Commons about trades-unionism. When the kaiser asked him if trades-unionism in England lead to frequent breeches of contract or rioting, Mr. Burt was able to assure his majesty that breach of contract was practically unknown, and that rioting seldom or never occurred. He further stated that they had solved that problem by freedom; that when the laws against combination existed there was some violence; but since the men had been left free to combine and do their business in their own way there had been none, while great improvement had been secured in the social condition of the workmen."

Commenting upon the interview between the emperor and Mr. Burt, W. T. Stead, editor of the *Review of Reviews*, wrote:

" It was worth while holding the Labor Conference, if only that Thomas Burt might have the opportunity of speaking such words of sound sense in the ear of the Emperor of Germany."

Mr. Burt's father was a miner and a Primitive Methodist local preacher. In 1844 there was a great strike of the miners of Seghill. All who dwelt in the colliery proprietors' cottages were evicted, and Peter Burt, his wife, and little children were obliged to move. Says George Jacob Holyoake: "Peter Burt was, like his famous son in subsequent years, the last man to put himself forward, but the first to stand in the front when storm and stress came. Peter Burt was actively and prominently engaged in the strike, and when it became a question how the wageless miners were to live he was one of those who offered to become legally responsible for all goods obtained by them during their contest. In consequence of the conspicuous part he took in the dispute he was marked by refusal of employment after the strike was ended. Thomas Burt was then only in his seventh year, but he pondered these things. Subsequently his father was offered employment again, but in an ungracious way, and the old Pilgrim blood in his veins was stirred; he turned away, and migrated to the neighboring county of Durham." Peter Burt, says Mr. Holyoake, "belonged to the 'order of Rechabites;' so there was the example of prudence at home; the son went on his own conviction. A lecture he heard on temperance decided him to be an abstainer, a rule of conduct he considered 'calculated to develop whatever was highest and best in a man.' Those who are capable of being inspired by high ideals of public service, and cultivate manly habits, find meaner life ever after distasteful and impossible to them. This explains the singular and honorable career of Thomas Burt. His character was further formed by his father's connections. . . . He kept, what is a distinction and an advantage to possess, a 'prophets' chamber' in his house, and entertained the itinerant preachers who came his way. From their visits, and the wise and varied conversation that ensued, an observant listener like his son derived great advantage."

Next to Mr. Burt perhaps the most noted and influential leader of organized labor in England has been Joseph Arch, organizer and head of the Agricultural Laborers' Union, which has done more during the twenty-five years of its existence to improve the condition of the English peasant than any other agency. Mr.

Arch also was a local preacher, and became the peasants' leader because of their confidence in him and his known ability as a speaker and organizer. A writer in an American journal describes Mr. Arch as "the greatest in character and achievements, though not in learning, of all the English leaders." In his efforts he was aided by many other itinerant and local preachers; and it is an important fact that the call for the meeting at which the union was organized was almost wholly circulated over many miles of country by the Primitive Methodist preachers.

The first two parliamentary secretaries of the British Trades Congress were Methodists; and Henry Broadhurst, a working stone mason, who became the first workingman to hold a cabinet position in the English government, though not a full member, is actively identified with the educational and other important work of the Wesleyan Church, and in his house and with his cooperation was started the *Methodist Times.*

Among the Methodist laymen or local preachers who are prominently identified with the British labor movement are Charles Fenwick, who was a coal heaver when elected to Parliament, but possessed such ability as to be appointed parliamentary secretary of the British Trades Congress, and William Abraham, a miner, a famous Welsh bard, and until the last election the only non-English workingmen's member in Parliament.

The labor movement is more marked in England by religious leadership than in any other country in the world. This, as before stated, is largely due to the influence of Methodist laymen and local preachers. Had John Wesley ordered Thomas Maxfield to cease preaching, and thus deprived Methodism and the world of blessings that have resulted from the labors of local preachers, vastly different would have been the religious, social, and political history of England and indeed of the world.

Thorold Rogers, in *Six Centuries of Work and Wages*, says:

" I do not believe that the mass of peasants could have been moved at all had it not been for the organization of the Primitive Methodists, a religious system which, as far as I have seen its working, has done more good with scanty means, and perhaps, in some persons' eyes, with grotesque appliances for devotion, than any other religious agency."

And Principal Fairbairn, in his volume on *Religion in History and Modern Life*, discussing the estrangement of the working classes from the Church and the responsibility of the Church therefor, says :

" Methodism, in its several branches, has done more for the conversion and reconciliation of certain of the industrial classes to religion than any other English Church. It is but just to say that the enfranchisement of our mining and agricultural populations made this evident —that their regulative ideas were religious rather than utilitarian and secular. The politician finds, when he addresses the peasantry, that he has to appeal to more distinctly ethical and religious principles than when he addresses the upper or middle classes. And we may hope that even in a politician the principles he appeals to may ultimately affect his policy. Meanwhile, we simply note that it is the local preacher rather than the secularist lecturer who has, while converting the soul, really formed the mind of the miner and laborer, and who now so largely represents the ideas he seeks, in his dim and inarticulate way, to see applied to national policy and legislation."

The testimony of Principal Fairbairn to the interest of Methodism in the industrial classes is true to-day as in the past. No great strike has occurred in recent years that the workers have not found a friend in such Methodist leaders as Rev. Hugh Price Hughes and other ministers and laymen. When the striking coal miners two years ago, and the slate workers in

the quarries of Lord Penrhyn a year ago, sent
delegations to London to solicit aid for the
suffering men and their families, the delegations were provided for in Methodist homes,
and arrangements were made for them to present their cause from Methodist pulpits.   And
such aid is rendered to suffering humanity
whether the strike be approved or not.

VII.

AMERICAN METHODISM AND THE LABOR MOVEMENT OF TO-DAY.

METHODISM still is, as it has been since its preachers first proclaimed a free Gospel, the Church of and for the masses. But with changed conditions of society the Church in America has not kept as closely in touch with working people as it should have done. It is a singular fact that, while no Methodist workingman has come to the front as a religious labor leader, two of the most radical extremists and atheistic leaders were formerly Methodists. Samuel Fielding, one of the Chicago anarchists, who was sent to the penitentiary and afterward pardoned, was at one time a local preacher, and his power as a speaker was, in a large measure, doubtless due to his experience in preaching. The other, in another city, a so-called anarchist, whose bitterness of speech was due to the cruel blacklisting of which he was a victim, was formerly a Bible class teacher in a Methodist Sunday school. The tone of the utterances of both these men

would have been different, and perhaps they
would not have lost their faith in God and in
Jesus Christ as a personal Saviour, had they
been in constant touch with ministers and
brethren who appreciated the industrial conditions of which they were the victims, and sympathized with them in the motive which
prompted their efforts to improve those conditions, even though they could not indorse their
methods.

No doubt there are elements in our large
cities whose aims are a source of danger to society. Some of the leaders are, indeed, enemies of law and order. The influence of these
extremists over the mass of the people, however, is due chiefly to the fact that the working people are ignored by those who are called
the " upper classes," and that they come into
intellectual and social contact only with those
who would array them against existing conditions. If the " masses " are dangerous, as
many believe, is it the part of wisdom to per-
mit them to plot in secret against society?
On the contrary, would it not be wise to get
into personal touch with them and show them
that all are brothers—that the interest of each
is the interest of all? Only those who have
done this know how welcome such fraternal

interest is, and how much influence it gives to those who manifest it.

There is little doubt that the great Pullman strike was brought to a close at least a day sooner than it otherwise would have been through the influence of the Rev. W. H. Carwardine, the Methodist pastor at Pullman, Ill., who was regarded by the strikers in that place, many of whom were members of his church, as their friend. It is reasonable to assume, also, that the workingmen of Cincinnati will always believe they have friends in Dr. D. H. Moore, editor of the *Western Christian Advocate*, who presided, and Rev. J. W. Magruder and Rev. Gervase Roughton, the Methodist preachers who spoke at the public meeting held in that city in behalf of the coal miners whose families were suffering for food during the strike of 1897. And they will also feel assured that the Methodist Episcopal Church is their friend because of the fact that the Methodist Book Concern tendered the use of its building for the reception of supplies for the relief of the miners.

Perhaps the greatest need in America to-day is a leader who will possess the wisdom to conceive and the power to execute plans that will aid Christian workingmen to infuse a religious tone into the labor movement.   Such a leader will arise, and he may arise in the Methodist Church.   Indeed, there are a number of our ministers and members whose study of the great social problems of the day and whose work give promise that before long the leader desired will be found.   He will be, not an agitator, but a prophet of God, who will realize and fearlessly proclaim the gospel that Christ came to save both the individual and society, and that both are saved only through righteous life and conduct.   This involves more than many seem to think.   It is often said that " the minister should confine himself to preaching the simple Gospel of Christ."   That is true, but the simple Gospel of Christ relates to everything that affects the welfare of man.

The labor question is not a temporary issue, one that will be settled in a day.   It is a movement, and it is a part of the evolution of society.   Dr. Abel Stevens, the historian of Methodism, in an article in *Zion's Herald* on the labor problem, wrote :

" Indisputably this question is to be the next great problem of the race ; or, rather, it has already become the supreme and irrepressible question of the social and political world. There will inevitably be much friction, perhaps some disastrous abrasion, in the process of its evolution. . . . But it is a normal problem; it comes up legitimately in the progress of civilization; and, in spite of deplorable temporary accompaniments, it will be one of those grand strides, forward and upward, by which humanity has been achieving its glorious destiny; for glorious that destiny must be, according to the most obvious conditions and the constantly augmenting capabilities of the race, even apart from its best religious predictions on the subject. Prince Bismarck is reported to have lately expressed his conviction of the beneficent tendency of the problem. It has arisen, he said substantially, in the natural evolution of history; it is one of those antagonisms which develop humanity. I think we may advance farther, and (surprising as it may be to some readers) affirm that the problem is eminently a *Christian* fact—a necessary evolution of Christian ethics and of our Christian civilization, notwithstanding the avowed skepticism and anarchism of many of its leading agitators and organizations in both Europe and America. I venture even to assert that it is exclusively a product of Christian thought; and this is an aspect of the subject that seems hardly to have attracted the attention of the ever-increasing thinkers who are agitating the world about it."

Dr. Stevens also believed that this movement will eliminate, or at least absorb, most other great questions of the time—the questions of mercantile and financial legislation, of protection and free trade, incorporated capital, trusts, nationalism, individualism, etc.—and will abolish war between nations.

The preacher, whose divine message is for both capitalist and workingman, is still, as he has always been, the most powerful leader of thought; and, whether he wishes to do so or not, he must take part in the discussion of the social questions, which, as Dr. Stevens says, are a necessary evolution of our Christian civilization. He must not be a partisan, seeing only one side of these questions. He should thoroughly inform himself—to do which requires wide reading and personal intercourse with people of all classes—and in the spirit of Christ dispassionately, kindly, and in the fear of God alone, present the truth to rich and poor, capitalist and workingman alike, as occasion seems to require—as did John Wesley.

THE END.